The Finality Of

FRUITCAKE

A Collection Of Short Tales

Brian Gueyser

Kids At Heart Publishing LLC
PO Box 492
Milton, IN 47357
765-478-5773
www.kidsatheartpublishing.com

First published by Kids At Heart Publishing LLC 6/30/22
ISBN # 978-1-95662-808-1
Library of Congress Control Number: 2022908432

Published in Milton, IN

The books at Kids At Heart Publishing feature turn the page technology. No batteries or charging required.

8-956628-10-4

The author would like to express great thanks and appreciation to the following individuals for their valuable time and contributions in proofreading the tales in this collection:

Alysha Oglesby
Kayla Stump
Van Temple

Table of Contents

Opus Dei –Opus Estranged

Opus Dei—Opus Estranged

Julian turned the key and listened to the ancient lock click its resistance. He paused and took a deep breath before grasping the doorknob...he wasn't sure if he could really do this. He closed his eyes and swallowed, prayer on his lips for comfort. A rush of air greeted him as he entered. The room smelled warm, and faintly musty...the way a bedroom smells in the morning before it's been aired out. He stood in the doorway for just a moment, observing, taking in the little world before his eyes.

It was a standard room, with just enough space for a bed, a small bookcase, a desk, and a closet which held three robes, and a few sets of trousers with matching shirts. This was the sum of worldly possessions each man who lived here owned. On the desk was a pencil, along with a few pages of soft, memo-pad paper lain strewn. The bed—so neatly made—was undisturbed, as was everything else in the room...preserved, frozen in time as if nothing had happened. It was Brother Francisco who found him.

The three days prior to that morning, Brother Dominic had spoken to Brother Francisco for some length, complaining of stomach troubles. As such, his absence from morning prayer was to be expected...the empty place at breakfast no cause for alarm. But when he did not come down to lunch, Julian began to feel uneasy. There was no real reason, just a feeling in the pit of his stomach that he couldn't shake...a feeling of unease…foreboding. He asked the others, but no one had seen Brother Dominic that morning. Apparently, he didn't show up for work at the library either. Brother Wallace then told him that Brother Francisco had gone to check on him. Brother Francisco was the monastery doctor of sorts. An MD with fifteen years of experience, he had first come ten years ago, saying medicine as it was practiced left him feeling empty and unsatisfied. He was a kind and patient man with a subtle sense of humor, who was fond of gardening and reading. His small mouth always seemed slightly curved up in a smile…except for that morning.

Julian traveled the distance from the dining room to the monks' quarters with quick steps. He couldn't explain it, but something inside compelled him to hurry; the same feeling which accosted him the entire morning. He climbed the stairs and rounded the corner, entering the hallway where most of the brothers lived. On the far end of the hall, one door was open. It was very quiet, and as he neared, he felt the hair on his arms and neck begin to rise. He was perhaps three steps away when Brother Francisco stepped out into the hall looking tired, and somehow grave. When he saw Julian, something in his eyes changed—panic—and he quickly moved to intercept him.

"Brother Sebastian," he said hastily, holding a hand out to Julian's chest, almost as if to push him away, "Would you kindly call the Abbot?"

Julian's blood went cold in his veins. He started to protest, but Brother Francisco cut him off, "Or perhaps some water, eh? Would you be kind enough to fetch us some water?"

Something about the way his voice trembled, something about the way his eyes seemed brimmed with tears set off an alarm.

"What's happened?" Julian demanded.

At this, Brother Francisco's eyes fell to the carpet below. "Julian," he said softly, hand reaching up to clasp his shoulder, "I know you were very close...I'm afraid something serious has happened."

To hear his given name used at such a time was enough to guess at the horror which awaited in the room beyond, and he pushed past the doctor.

"Dominic!" he called out standing in the doorway.

The curtains were still drawn and the room was very dim, but he could make out the shape of someone in bed. As he stepped closer, he could see the blankets were well over the sleeper's head. However, most disturbing was the sleeper's eerie stillness. There was no sound, or movement. Not even the rhythmic movement of his breathing.

"Erin," he said, hearing the trembling in his voice. He knelt by the bed and shook him, calling louder, "Erin!"

He tried to speak again, but no sound would come. He sniffled and wiped at his tears as he pulled the blankets back from Erin's head. There, looking for all the world as if he were asleep, was Erin. His face looked peaceful, and it seemed at any moment his eyelids would flutter open and he'd laugh in that embarrassed way he liked to laugh and give some excuse about oversleeping. Julian hugged the body of his friend and wept. It was still warm…had he come a little earlier perhaps…perhaps…. He felt the doctor's hand stroking his back.

Julian roused himself from his memory, taking a breath to settle his nerves, and forced his eyes from the bedside of his friend where he had wept so. He gave his leg a pat and nodded his head. Mind set with the task at hand, the first thing he did was open the curtains. Then, with light sufficiently filling the room, he decided to open the window. The air was cool and brisk. It entered the room gracefully, playfully fretting and turning the corners as if stretching long, cramped legs. He removed the sheets for laundering, and placed them in a pile on the desk. He then retrieved the broom he had brought with him, and began the task of sweeping the floor. During this time, he couldn't help but think of all the times he and Erin had talked in this very room… or laughed…or shared their deepest secrets with each other.

He had come to the monastery two years before, Erin three. They had become friends quickly—at first more a result of circumstances—later recognizing the traits they had in common. Erin was the reluctant monk. He loved to sleep, and as a result was always late to morning Lauds. He also hated studying, and more often than not would find his way into something or other during self-enrichment time. He often spent this time in the library—while he hated studying per se, he enjoyed researching—looking up things which sparked his interest. Sometimes, he found his way to Julian's room, and they would talk about anything and everything. At the same time, he was never a nuisance…always very respectful of privacy.

They always used their given names when talking with each other...their ordination names a thing forgotten and unbecoming. Julian was the serious one. Straight out of college with the intention of going to seminary, his entrance to the monastery had been a way to reaffirm his resolve. From day one he knew he had made the right decision, and immersed himself in learning the ways of the brotherhood.

His meeting with "Brother Dominic" had come a month after he had arrived at the monastery; his first time at kitchen duty. He arrived at 6:45a.m., fifteen minutes early, to familiarize himself with the kitchen and its equipment. He was thoroughly disappointed to discover the building was still dark, and in fact still locked. Twenty-five minutes later he heard the fluttering of robes and the panting of a monk who had been running. He was a man of average build and height—or so it seemed through the habit—with short red hair. He hurriedly opened the door, and began shouting orders as he scrambled here and there gathering pots, and spoons and pans and ingredients. Breakfast went off with no major problems, and despite the general chaos of the situation, they worked smoothly and efficiently together. As they finished preparing the food, he introduced himself as, "Brother Dominic—but you can call me Erin".

If pressed to give a first impression, Julian would have chosen the word "haphazard", or "disorganized" to describe Brother Dominic. The second day of kitchen duty went similar to the first, with Brother Dominic dashing through the courtyard towards the door and Julian standing beside it. By the second week, he was wise enough to give Julian the keys. With this newfound freedom he was able to sleep in slightly later, and Julian was also able to familiarize himself with the kitchen, its ancient ovens, refrigerators, and scores and scores of cookbooks. Their last day of duty together, right before the monthly rotation, Julian arrived to find the kitchen lights on, and the smell of something wonderful wafting from the windows. As he went in, he discovered—to his surprise—Brother Dominic hovering above something brown and ring-shaped. He beamed a smile as Julian stepped in the door.

"You're just in time Sebs, you get to try the first piece", he said.

With that, he handed Julian a slice of something. Julian hesitated before tasting it, but once he had, he was amazed at the perfection of flavor. It could have easily been the subject of some famous, upscale restaurant.

He glanced his question at Brother Dominic, who in turn answered, "To celebrate the success of your first kitchen duty".

The pastry was apparently Scandinavian, and they even toasted with a small bit of white wine, which Brother Dominic produced from some secret hiding place.

"Congratulations, Brother Sebastian," Brother Dominic said raising his glass.

Julian smiled, returning the toast, "Julian...my name is Julian", he replied.

As he paused, glancing around the empty room as if in search of some hidden harbor of sanctuary, Julian felt his eyes begin to well with tears again. It was funny the way these memories could hurt so much, and yet make him smile so. He squeezed the rag and watched the water splash into the bucket. Once again, he brought it over the window, taking care to get the corners. As he finished, he folded a piece of old newspaper and polished the glass until it seemed to shine. This finished, he made his way towards the closet. As he opened the door, a familiar scent greeted his nose, and his breath caught in his throat. It was funny how even the clothes a person wore carried their scent. The garments were scarce, but each one precious because they held within them the life of the man who had used them. These would need laundering as well. Julian took each robe from its hanger and folded it with care, almost as if preparing them for a long, long journey. He set them on the bed, and then decided to sit and rest.

It had been three weeks since the funeral, and someone needed to clean the room. Since they had been so close, it seemed only right that he should be the one to set things in order. But now that he was face to face with the task, it seemed a bit overwhelming. How could he be expected to pick up the pieces left behind, and then continue on as if nothing had ever happened? How could he be apprentice to a process which would erase all trace of Erin's existence there? He sighed remembering...it hadn't all been happy. Had it been a month ago, two?? He couldn't remember exactly, but on that day, Erin knocked softly on his door. He opened it expecting news of some new scheme or discovery, but instead was greeted by the sight of a sad, sad man.

"Erin, what happened?" he asked him, closing the door, studies forgotten.

Erin sat on the bed and put his head in his hands. He began to speak twice, and then without warning burst into tears. Julian did everything he could think of to try to comfort him, but he wouldn't stop. He wasn't sure what to do, or if he should go and get someone to help him, so instead he sat beside him and held him. He held him a long time that night. It was the first time he held another man. When they met the next day, Erin smiled meekly, and laughed it all off as if it were no big deal. But from that time on, Julian began to notice something strange. Erin seemed withdrawn, and as if his mind was elsewhere. He went to prayer, but he sat sullenly in the pew farthest from anyone else, and hardly said a word.

Brother Ignacious, the eldest of the brothers, dismissed it as nothing but a phase.

"Every monk goes through it at some time or other… questions of life, death, faith. He's probably asking himself is this what he really wanted in life, and if he made a mistake. Either that or he's fallen in love and is wondering whether he should quit things here for a life of marriage". Then he shook his head and chuckled, "I've been down that road before…and seen it all too many times in my years".

The other brothers seemed concerned, but not overtly worried. This being the case, Julian didn't feel as if voicing his own doubts would serve any use. He remembered the last time he had talked to Erin. He'd decided to try and cheer him up, and had thought all day about what he could do. In the end, he decided cooking him something would be a good start. He remembered Erin talking about how he loved Indian food one day, and so he decided he would try to make samosas. It was his first time, so there was no real way to know what he was doing, but when he saw the way Erin's face lit up after seeing them, he knew he had done something right. They ate, and talked about nothing in particular, Erin laughing softly as if to ease his way back into the habit again. It all went well until the end of the meal, when Erin's face suddenly went blank.

"That's the best thing I've eaten in a long time...I'm just so tired lately...I just want to rest," he said.

They cleared the dishes in silence, Julian washing, Erin drying. They were just drying their hands when Erin suddenly grasped his shoulder.

"Thank you for doing this, I really appreciate it."

Julian tried not to betray his concern through his smile. "Are you going to be alright?" he'd asked.

Erin didn't answer right away, but instead gave his shoulder a pat and smiled. "I think I'm going to go to bed now. I'll see you tomorrow."

Something about his voice sounded hollow and afraid, and made Julian want to grab his hand and have him tell him what was going on. But he did none of this, watching silently as Erin closed the door behind himself.

The clouds blew slowly across the sky, tracing vague patterns of wind and light. He wondered had the clouds looked this way to Erin right before he took those pills. The empty bottle lay on the floor near the bed. He was confused when he first saw it. Why was this bottle here and what happened to its contents? He looked back and forth between the bottle and Erin's body, forcing himself to conclude that which he didn't want to believe. Suicide.

The Abbot had been quite disturbed, and particularly saddened when he heard the news. Suicide was hard to accept in any case, but for those of the brotherhood it was unthinkable. For those whose lives were devoted to that which was most holy and sanctified to take their lives into their own hands seemed akin to blasphemy. At the funeral service, Brother Bartholomew gave the most beautiful eulogy, though through tears. And there wasn't a dry eye in the choir. The service all and all was comforting, and no one mentioned damnation or eternal suffering...it was apparent Erin had suffered enough in life. Julian himself said very little, though the Abbot himself had requested him to say a few words. Truthfully, he did not know what to say. What could he possibly say to the man he had failed...he was sorry he didn't listen? Should he say he wished he had trusted his feeling of unease and come to see him that morning... maybe in time to save him? Should he talk about the bonds of friendship that he felt between them—even now—and how they had become a part of each other's lives? In truth, he could say nothing because anything he tried to say seemed empty and unimportant to him.

The sun shone down into the small little room, warming its corners, newly cleaned floor, and neatly made bed. Julian surveyed his work, thinking to himself. He had finished cleaning and had even changed the sheets. Each small detail changed and somehow made anew. Who now would occupy this room he did not know. He only hoped and prayed that in keeping the Divine Office, they would find more comfort, more peace, and more solace than Erin ever had.

Sojourner

Brian Gueyser

Sojourner

When I first see Eric's face, it's as if all the years between us melt away, and we're left with nothing but our love and how we used to be. That's it. That's how I'd like to like to remember him. That's how I'd like us to remember each other...days of shimmering airborne whirligigs, and tamarind tasting afternoons spent by the pier...or in the shade of that huge oak tree in his backyard. It's the things like these I'd like to remember, and let the rest fade away as if it never was....as if it were the mist of a deep winter's night cringing back in upon itself at the first piercing shard of daylight. Yes, this is how I'd like to be able to remember us. Instead, I'm left with bruises and scars, broken-hearted dreams and songs whose notes I can't quite remember. I know it's not his fault per se—not really—but even as I look into his eyes now, I feel the bitter anger and resentment begin to seethe and slowly rise into my belly.

"Hullo," he says to me, looking sheepishly cute and awkwardly adorable in his tan Rumpelstiltskin sweater.

He'd always call it that because everyone would always ask him what the embroidered letters near the collar meant. He'd often joke that he'd have to kill them if he told them.

"Eric," I say, breath catching in my throat.

"I see you're well," he continues, hardly giving me time to think, let alone consider how I should tell him what he obviously hasn't understood. "Look, I know

I've been distant lately," he starts, hand running through his hair…still as disheveled, still as curly, still as wonderfully springy and shiny as I remember it…yet the light here somehow capturing a quality of luminosity I've never known, as if each and every fibre stretched out into the world to taste each thing and know it by name. "And I really want to come with you to Zanzibar, I really do," he continues, leaning on his shovel, oblivious to the way the wind should feel against our skin as it rustles the trees behind him, or the way the dirt road beneath us seems at once to be made of dry red clay, and spongy earthen smiles. "But Zanzibar's such a…a…well, a change. And I for one cannot afford to start with something so drastic at this stage in my life right now," he finishes.

How is it that this man's eyes are so green? And if his eyes are so full of life to me here, I wonder how I must look to him.

"I'm only just a few months from a major breakthrough. I can feel it!" he says to me, looking so excited and so proud…but somehow also so worn and weary and fragile…just like the last time I saw him, wondering if he'd be happy so many people would see him in his "tweed imitation-professor-suit" as he used to call it.

He takes a breath and looks at me as if I were a child too small to understand complex words. He looks away towards his excavation tools—strewn about the side of the road near his toolbox—before facing me once more.

"So I'm sorry," he finally breathes out, "but I don't think we can continue to see each other."

How is it that he can't understand that things are different now...so, utterly and completely different? My eyes fill with tears and he closes the distance between us easily and effortlessly, not taking the time to notice how even his long legs shouldn't move so quickly; not noticing the silence of the shovel striking the soft red rocky earth.

"I really am sorry," he says, hand reaching out to touch my shoulder, "I do love you. I really do. But I think...I think perhaps we're just not...compatible... enough," he mutters awkwardly, staring at the ground which shifts and sways and seems to be echoing whatever it is he's feeling.

How I wish he would take a moment—just a moment—to think things through. Maybe then he'd notice the way the trees seem to be at odds with one another, or that his clothes seem remarkably clean for a man who's been digging all day, or that he's packed no lunch and he has nowhere to sleep. But he's still stuck here with his one-track mind, his research, and his nomination for professorship. I throw my arms around him, lunging into a hug and take him by surprise. I hear his gasp clearly, but cannot feel his ribs expanding as he takes in the air. I kiss him on the cheek, then move back to look him directly in the eyes.

"Happy Valentine's Day Eric. Happy Valentine's... and, goodbye," I say.

You'd think it would hurt...at least a little. Perhaps it would have at one time. He gives a small smirk, and then moves to collect his shovel.

"Eric please just leave it where it is. You don't have

to do that anymore," I say, hoping I don't sound as exasperated as I feel with this entire situation.

He looks at me as if I've lost my mind.

"Your research is over, and there's no point in you being here. You'll have to apply somewhere else to teach," I say, wondering if I truly feel as crestfallen as I sound.

Suddenly his eyes grow cold and stony; when he next speaks his voice is stern and sullen.

"I see. You've come to pick fights again. Haven't I already told you I'm sorry?" he says testily.

"Oh Eric," I say, voice falling, "No...no you aren't understanding, Eric. You don't understand. I came here to help you," I reply.

"Do what? Dig?" he asks, looking bemused.

I open my mouth to begin to respond, then stop. This isn't as easy as I imagined it would be.

"Eric you're dead," I say gently, "You've died Eric...you've been dead almost three years now. In my dreams I've seen you in this place digging and digging...always just digging. So I came to do something about it," I say to him, trying my best to convey the message as clearly as possible without shattering his reality completely.

I cannot interpret the look I see cross his face. It begins at one end, then shifts clear across to the other in a slow, undulating wave that distorts his brow and steals the glimmer from his eyes for just a moment before he replies.

"That's funny," he remarks, eyes at his feet before they leap to meet mine, glittering with something akin to excitement. "I have a shadow," he says, seeming all at once amused by this new and interesting game yet utterly triumphant in the display of his superior intellect.

He draws my gaze down with his towards the shadow beneath him, and when I look at him again, I notice the way the ends of his mouth have curled up into a smile...thin, pink lips seeming just as soft and delicately sensuous as they were the last time we kissed.

"I don't," I reply softly, then before he can speak, "and Eric where is the sun?"

"What do mean where's the sun?" he asks, looking at me like I'm ridiculous, then swivels his head towards the sky this way and that, beard shining like coiled shards of flame. "Well," he begins, "Since my shadow's casting this way, it must logically be..." he trails off, seeming confused for just a moment before beginning again, cupping his hands over his eyebrows to shield them; this time sounding more irritated "Or... well I mean I can't actually look into the sun you know...it's just...it's just so bright is all—" he finishes.

"Of course it's bright. There's light all around us," I say matter of factly, raising my voice and cutting him off. "But where is that light coming from?"

He looks at me again, this time lips pressed together tightly.

"I don't know why you're doing this. This doesn't mean anything, and I don't care to fight with you again.

I'm busy. And if there's nothing else, I'd like you to go," he says, sounding more disappointed than defeated.

"Eric look at me," I say as gently as I can imagine. "You don't have to stay here. There is no here...this is something you've created with your mind."

He frowns silently down at me.

"How hot is it today?" I ask suddenly. His eyebrow rises and he has absolutely no idea why this is important.

"I don't know, maybe 40?" he says with a shrug.

"Alright, take off your shirt," I continue.

He smirks and opens his mouth to say something, then seems to think the better of it and complies. It only takes him a moment to remove his jacket, and he holds it oddly between his legs as he unfastens his shirt's buttons. He whips the shirt off and thrusts it at me defiantly, as if daring me to find fault with him or his logic. I take it from his hand and give it a good hard shake; noting the way it snaps crisply and cleanly as I do.

"If it's really 40, and you've really been out here digging—what all day?—then why isn't your shirt drenched with sweat?" I ask.

The smirk on his face fades slowly as he looks from me to the shirt, then back again. I turn the shirt this way and that, examining it myself as well as giving him ample opportunity to take in exactly what I'm showing him.

"It's not even damp," I tell him, "And how long have you been out here digging?"

He looks away, trying his hardest to think…to remember. He knows he can't be wrong and yet somehow, something just doesn't seem to add up.

"I…don't…know," he admits finally, eyes sweeping the scene around him…the hole he's made, his tools, the very landscape where we stand. He stands this way a long time, face alternating between a look of panic and mild dismay. "But it feels so…." he says finally, trailing off.

"I know," I say softly.

His eyes scan the ground until they come to where my feet stand. He sees and understands for the first time that I truly cast no shadow here.

Suddenly his eyes are upon me again, filled with tears and a pleading urgency.

"You have no shadow," he says, "You have no shadow, my God why don't you have a—is this—are we both—am I…did I really…die?" he asks me, voice diminishing into itself as if it were an insect afraid of being squashed.

I place both of my hands on his shoulders and nod. He looks down at his feet—or mine, I cannot tell—then raises his head as if still searching for the nonexistent sun, before facing me again.

"Were we…" he begins gingerly, "alright?" he asks, voice quivering as if he's too afraid to hear the answer.

I should tell him the truth. Now of all times I should speak only the truth and finally set things right between us.

"No Eric," I hear my voice whisper, "No, we were not okay," I manage to eke out before the tears come.

He closes his eyes, face contorting with a pained look, before he asks me, "How did this happen?"

"Eric we were fighting, and you stormed out of the house," I say sobbing. "They said when they found you you'd been drinking, and when you left the bar you just stepped out into the street. The driver didn't see you, and he couldn't—" I begin to explain before the tears overcome my voice again.

"Shhh, it's okay," I hear him murmur at me; scooping me into a bear hug of an embrace just like he used to.

We stay like this for some time before he speaks again. "And you came here...for me?"

I nod into his shoulder.

"Thank you," I hear his voice quaver.

He steps back and holds me by the shoulders, looking at me like he used to when we were certain that our love above all others was eternal.

"Now what?" he whispers, neither looking as frightened nor as confident as he did just mere seconds ago.

I point to the narrow path between the trees behind him. He turns to regard it for a moment or two, then turns and looks at where his tools lay scattered about on the soil.

"I don't suppose I'll be needing those then will I," he says, half-jokingly to himself.

He turns towards the path and takes a step or two

before turning towards me. He reaches out his hand and smiles. I move towards him, and place my hand within his.

We mostly speak of nothing as we walk along the path; noticing the different varieties of trees, and the strange and lovely birds. Sometimes the path grows until it seems it is the only thing which exists, and other times it becomes so narrow we have to walk one in front of the other. Through it all, he never lets my hand go. Sometimes he embraces me for a moment or two, and other times he just smiles at me as I step along side of him. When we leave the trees and begin to approach the bridge, I know he has to cross it alone. I slow my pace as the land begins to swell with a few gentle rolling slopes before evening out once more. He looks at me confused, then gives my hand a tug, but I do not budge. He looks at the bridge, then back at me, and smiles.

"I suppose…this…is it then…huh?" he says, more to himself than anything.

I take his shirt from where I'd tucked it in at my waist and place it on him now, fastening each button slowly and methodically. I brush it off once or twice, then step back and give him a once over.

He closes the distance between us and has my face in his hands, "You came for me," he says softly.

I smile up at him. "Of course I did," I say, wishing I were clever enough to say something moving, wishing I were brave enough to tell him what I've wished I could have told him before he walked away that night three years ago.

He pulls me into an embrace, kisses me on the forehead, and then lets go. He's not stepped up onto the bridge before he's turned to look at me again.

"You deserve better than to wait patiently for someone to love you," he says, "I hope Zanzibar is more than you could possibly imagine."

Part of me instinctively moves to correct him, but I catch myself, and leave it be. I smile weakly. There are no long moments of farewell, and there is no final understanding which silently passes between us. For a short time, we are simply there, bearing witness to one another as we truly are. Eric doesn't look back again after crossing, and I'm left alone; with earth scorched red as my heart.

The Finality Of Fruitcake

The Finality Of Fruitcake

Samantha rounded the corner and took a few slow deep breaths as she neared the bakery. It wasn't that she was disappointed per se. It just seemed rather…plain. She pursed her lips and swatted at a stray strand of hair as she sized it up. When compared to the buildings around it, the bakery almost seemed antiquated…and she wondered how it had survived all these years in such a location. True, she thought to herself with a rise of an eyebrow, she was no expert in London's realty scene by any means; in fact, she'd only just arrived in the city six hours prior. Still, she liked to imagine herself at least somewhat knowledgeable in a vast array of subjects; with much more than the commonly feigned familiarity of the workings of the social world.

"That's what I like about you," Athena had said to her once. "The pursuit of trivial seeming knowledge sparks a flare of excitement in you—I can always see it in your eyes y'know—and I think that's cute."

Samantha felt her lips curl into the slightest of smiles as her hand moved gingerly to her left front coat pocket. She located the plastic sandwich bag quickly, and moved it deftly, so that only one corner was exposed. She gingerly opened and inserted two fingers in one fluid movement, and pinched a tiny piece—for her purposes, this was all she required—before bringing her fingers to her mouth. As she savoured the taste of the fruitcake, she allowed the tears to gently well in her eyes.

Athena was a master of fruitcake. Though a reference librarian by profession, she excelled at the creation of confectionaries, and the fruitcake, was her pièce de résistance. Like most people she knew, Samantha had never given fruitcake a fair chance to make an impression; always relegating it to that category of bothersome gifts bequeathed to acquaintances, irritating neighbours, and community busy-bodies. But with Athena's fruitcake, the combination of flavours caressed her tongue and made her senses reel and dance in delight!

Samantha could never quite figure out what it was precisely, whether it was the way the velvety soft cake slipped silently across her palate…or the way the fruit teased her tongue with tart timbers of delicate sweetness. Perhaps it was the texture, or the taste of the nuts: rich and robust. Or was it the brandy? The wine? The fruit juice in which it had been soaked? Whatever it was, she found herself wrapped within its spell within moments…the world slipping away until it was only the two of them, held in the warmth of their love. It happened each time she indulged—and indulge she did often; savouring each sweetly sectioned sliver. This time, as she allowed her taste-buds more and the world around her faded, for a moment there was no bakery, there was no darkened city or cold and foreign night. There were no tears, there was no panged longing, and there was no sorrow. For in these moments Athena still lived, and the distance that separated them was only as near as the next mouthful.

She couldn't exactly say when she began her quest. Perhaps it was some time after the second year…it may have well been the anniversary of the third. But she was almost certain that it happened after she found herself in a bakery in San Francisco. The conference she'd been attending was done for the day, and she was left wandering the streets and taking in the city.

It was by chance that she stumbled across the bakery, and at a whim that she allowed herself to enter. As a rule, she did not enjoy desserts, and especially since Athena's death she'd avoided them at all costs—for she was certain they could only pale in comparison to her mastery. When she found the fruitcake, she was startled. The clerk asked if she was alright, and she nodded silently; smiling her thanks. She only hesitated a moment, then purchased a piece and fled.

Only once safely in the private sanctuary of a park did she allow herself to unravel the parchment paper wrapping. When she saw it, she gasped. There it was. Heavy. The weight of it in her palm like the unspoken weight of grief on her heart. She brought the cake to her nose and gave a tentative sniff. Perfume-y. When she tasted it, she imagined aristocratic pageantry and elitist social gatherings with far too little substance and guests who'd had far too much to drink. She couldn't finish it. She left it there on the bench as she returned to her hotel, tossing and turning all night with the taste of betrayal on her lips. She was so relieved when she returned home that first thing she did was run to the cupboard and unwrap the first of the last three fruitcakes Athena had ever made. As she stared at it—bringing her face so close that its scent permeated her every breath—she burst into tears.

Samantha had never noticed the way the quiet reference librarian smiled at her before. She'd never bothered to note the way her eyes seemed to sparkle or her smile seemed to brighten whenever she came near; never addressing her directly, but waiting…waiting to be of service. So, she'd only been slightly taken aback the day she'd asked her over for coffee and cake. Not being fond of desserts to begin with, Samantha's first impulse was to politely refuse. But for some reason, as she gazed into those warm and glittering pools of amber light, she heard her voice accept.

Athena's home was large and spacious. The wood furnishings stark and powerful, yet somehow comforting against the soft toned carpets and mildly hued decorations. Her living room was full of books. There were shelves upon shelves, and each one filled to the brim. Yet, they were neatly and quite precisely arranged—as Samantha would discover months later after they'd started dating, and she'd carelessly placed a literary anthology in the section relegated to cookbooks and world cuisine. The fruitcake, the first time she had it—that very first bite—took her breath away. And like much of their life afterwards, she would never understand its simple power to pervade and persuade the very course of her desires.

Long committed to memory, Athena had no need of a recipe to make it. She knew instinctively which spice came when. They'd been together six years… and Samantha had cherished each and every one of them. As their burgeoning relationship matured, she soon discovered that Athena—just like the Goddess for which she was named—was a true trove of wisdom. She relished their lazy Sunday afternoons where they'd snuggle against one another—Samantha dozing, head in Athena's lap as Athena read to her—and their

Saturday morning brunches. She loved to watch her in the kitchen…carefully selecting each ingredient and preparing it so thoughtfully yet effortlessly that before she knew it, the timer would be set, the oven would be closed, and she'd find herself gazing deep into the soul of the woman she knew beyond a shadow of a doubt that she would spend the rest of her life with.

The first year after her passing, Samantha tried in vain to replicate it, and was devastated when she failed. How, she wondered, could she have taken something so simple so much for granted that one day she awoke to find it gone? She visited the orchards they'd visited to select the finest nuts. She'd candied the fruit herself. She'd even gone three hours out of her way to find the best type of brandy. But in the end, she was only left with fleeting memories of a time when light was laughter, and patience was marked by the delicate wrapping of a fruitcake after it cooled.

Faced with the reality that Athena's fruitcake could not be duplicated, she hoarded what remained of it jealously, and partook of it sacredly. She found herself falling into a pattern: one slice on Christmas Eve, and one slice on New Year's Day. One slice on her birthday, and one slice on Athena's. She could not bring herself to eat it on the anniversary of her death, but around that time each year she found herself at a bakery, an orchard, or a market. Each time searching for the perfect combination of ingredients. Each time reaching into that shared ethereal realm of memory in the hope that suddenly she would somehow remember a word or phrase, some clue to aid her in the fruitcake's creation. Each time searching for a glimpse into the past where they'd been happy.

Somehow over the years the three fruitcakes became two, and the two became one until one day Samantha realized she was only left with less than half of the cake which was the signature dish of the woman she so loved. She needed it now like she needed Athena's touch; longed for it now as she longed for the rich tenor notes of her laughter. And so, like the faithful, predictable pilgrim she had become, she wound her way towards the little bakery tucked in-between anonymous business buildings in London.

The purpose of her journey here—on the surface— was of little importance. Oh, she'd filled out the immigration forms with the correct replies of course. But none of that had been significant. What truly mattered, was that Athena had liked London. She once told Samantha that she'd spent nearly an entire three days of an eight-day trip exploring the Bishopsgate Institute Library. And what better place, Samantha thought, to remember her this year than spending time in a place that she held dear?

When the bakery opened, Samantha was the first customer to go inside. She pretended to peruse the selections, knowing in her heart that she should cherish the fleeting feelings of hope before tasting the brash disappointment of disillusion. She purchased a slice, and slipped through the door before the sleepy clerk could wish her well. She still had some time before the library opened, and she leisurely strolled the streets, watching the city come to life. She purposely waited a few hours before arriving. She wanted the experience to be as it would be on any normal day—as much as it had been when Athena had been there.

As she entered the library doors, she detected the distinct odour of a multitude of books that only a library can possess. She stepped gingerly, enveloped and comforted in a world of silence that somehow— somehow connected her to a time and person who had made her heart leap and ring with songs of flame. The corner was unobtrusive and inviting, and Samantha knew that the spot was perfect the instant she saw it. As she sat, she took in the sights surrounding her; imagining what these very walls must have looked like through Athena's eyes. She unwrapped the forbidden morsel and boldly set it on the small table in plain sight. Not that anyone was near enough to see it, but the act alone made her feel courageous and heroic, as if she were the protagonist in one of the tales Athena read to her all those long Sunday afternoons ago.

When she tasted it, she wept. Wept for its inferior quality, wept for her stubborn naivety, and most of all wept for the solace encased within the flavours of a fruitcake she would—once it was gone—never know again.

She wasn't sure how long she had been weeping when suddenly she felt it. She felt it. What was life, but one hint of flavour melding with another? And what was love, but the careful, mindful wrapping of a relationship—and all of its details—in layer after layer of beautifully delicate intricacy. She laughed, giddy at the hint of all that seemed suddenly possible. She'd been searching for so long, holding on for so long. Perhaps in all her searching she'd neglected to tend to the flavours which enriched her own life.

She smiled, certain that she'd come to understand

something that day. She was certain that she'd still drop in to a bakery on occasion; certain that she'd still peruse its wares for that perfect slice of fruitcake…that slice that would transport her back to a time where she had loved and she was love. And though some part of her knew she'd never find it, she was still helpless to stop herself from searching for hints of her flavour in each city she visited…searching for a glimpse of her divine beauty in each bakery she entered.

Song Of Saeed

Song Of Saeed

1

[Present Day—Nepal]

The wind is warm today. It pushes gently against my back and scrapes against my ears…almost the way he used to. He's nervous. It is awkward. He stares at his hands which drum and fidget on the small, round table between us, grasping for something—anything—to occupy their attention. I examine the way dark wisps of hair on his fingers and hands—large, slim, confident and nimble hands, usually so certain of their strength—blend perfectly with the timbre of his rich complexion. Hands in my lap, I wait, patiently. The waiter sets our tea between us. I thank him and motion to Saeed. His eyes follow the movement of my hand—and the *mala* encircling my wrist—as I grasp the glass and move it closer, waiting for the scalding liquid to cool. He glances up quickly, mouth opening, and our eyes meet. This man has beautiful eyes. Warm pools of brightly lit amber shine back at me, clear…pure…inviting.

Though it happens very quickly, I am certain I detect a quiver—something akin to sound…waves smashed against glass—and they dart back towards the table. To come here has been very hard for him. This—if nothing else—is apparent from his manner. The way he refuses to look directly at me, the way he holds his body—far too tense—his quick, non-descript, vacant sentences used to anchor and terminate thoughts before they begin…a way of masking his emotions. Yes, this is very hard for him indeed, as it should be. Considering the circumstances of our parting, it's a wonder he even came at all.

Seeing him this way, being here now, I can't help but remember our last night together all those years ago. It was a very hard time then as well, and we were both very sad, though we did not weep. We were through with weeping. It came at odd moments during ordinary routines. It rocked us to sleep and awakened us to prayer each morning for three months prior...it was a time of momentous sorrow. That night he kept kissing me...small, warm pecks of love against my skin. He murmured—as he always did during lovemaking—yet this time he spoke one phrase continuously.

"Saeed," he murmured between kisses, "I am Saeed."

And I laid there that night on top of him quivering...quivering with anger and fear...also sadness... also love...as he kissed—marked—each spot upon this body with his lips and tasted me one final time with his tongue, took my scent into him through his nose, and ensnared me with his eyes. Those eyes, those beautiful eyes. It is those same eyes I attempt to gaze into sitting here now. Those same beautiful eyes which refuse to meet my own. His heavy brows furrow and I delight in wonder noticing newer creases and folds upon his aging skin. I look down to his chin with its perpetual five o'clock shadow and wonder are there flecks of grey. Surely there must be, I think, smiling; returning my gaze to the backs of my own hands.

To see him again is a good thing. It is funny, I am not angry. Neither am I embittered with rage nor heartbroken nor torn. I am curious…and you might even say that I am almost glad to see him…to see that he is—or seems anyway—physically healthy.

Two days ago, I had been in the temple sweeping. Our summer fasting *puja* had just finished and now—able to eat whenever we wanted—with a bit of a break in our regular schedule of prayer and study, the few of us left behind began to joke amongst ourselves about the various treats we would consume, and about which some of us had even dreamed so intensely while fasting. We were in the middle of such joking; bent over double with laughter, when little Tashi came running to see me. He was only seven, recently taken in as a novice, but he was so determined in his excitement that he nearly fell over when he bolted up the steps. This added to our amusement greatly.

"What's the hurry there little one?" I said to him as he skidded to a stop, panting.

"I saw…your friend," he said between breaths, "he gave me three sweets!"

"Three?!" I answered, trying to sound very impressed. This elicited another roar of laughter from the others.

"You'll rot out all your teeth!" Sonam teased him.

"Yea, and then we'll have to pull out all the bad ones, and you'll never be able to talk again!" added Lobsang with a devilish smile, hunching over slowly and extending his arms as if he were some evil monster bent on eating up little children.

Tashi jumped with pleasure, giggling while Lobsang hobbled closer and closer in his imitation mon-ster-style stalk. Things went on this way until Tashi decided to hide behind me. Apparently forgetting the contents of his hand, he grabbed the bottom part of my robe, sending a handful of candy and a crumpled up piece of paper crashing to the floor.

"Hey hey!" cried Dorje through smiles, "We've just tidied this up! Now we'll really have to pull out all your teeth for spreading rubbish around!"

Tashi began to bolt for the door shrieking, when he remembered his candy. He stopped midstep and came back full speed to retrieve it. He handed me the piece of paper before dashing off again.

"For you!" he called over his shoulder.

I frowned, shaking my head; watching him disap-pear.

"Oh to be his age again," I remarked to Lobsang, who had resumed sweeping. "And he carries around rubbish too, what am I to do with this?" I remark more to myself than anyone else.

"But it's not rubbish, it's from your 'friend' right?" said Dorje.

We all erupted into laughter. Why wouldn't anyone I knew come to me directly? The settlement wasn't that large to begin with, and the monastery was far from isolated.

"Right, then I suppose I should see what he wants then eh?" I quipped, opening the crumpled paper.

As I did so, it became apparent that this was indeed

from someone I knew…from someone I had known quite intimately. My heart jolted once against my breast quite powerfully, then became oddly still. My face fell, and became smooth and unexpressive. Detecting my sudden change in behaviour, the group became quiet.

"Are you okay?" Lobsang asked.

"I'm fine," I replied, wondering if I really sounded so.

He held out his hand to inspect the paper for himself. When he saw it, he erupted into smiles, passing it around.

"Aah, he is playing jokes! Don't mind!" The others agreed and we went back to our task.

It didn't take long to finish, and as we were putting the brooms away Dundup returned the paper to me, recognizing it for what it was.

"What does this say?" he asked gently, concern evident from the tone of his voice.

My mouth opened to reply, but for a moment no sound came forth. How do I tell him?

I cleared my throat and tried again, this time successfully, "It says someone I knew long ago has come to see me," I replied softly.

It was only then, as Dundup took hold of my hand, that I realized it had been trembling.

Saeed is trembling now I imagine, though I am not certain. His fingers drum the table more quickly now and he gathers his courage to speak. The lemon tea is still too hot but he takes two gulps, wincing from the heat. I watch his face contort in pain as he begins to cough and sputter. I am instantly out of my seat and I move to help him, but he moves his chair back, holding out one hand to wave me away. He quiets down and I sit. He mutters something about it being hot. What an understatement, I think sarcastically. In my mind, images of our life together twist and turn into bright echoes and laughter. How long were we together? Five? Ten years? How long had it been since we last saw each other? Another five, eight years? Could it really have been that long? Why does the past always seem so close? He speaks and brings me back to the present.

"I don't know how to begin," he says softly, voice trembling.

His voice is weighted with agony and I feel my eyes fill with tears. Without thinking I move to take his hands into my own, but he jerks them away. The shock, the pain has just enough time to register before—just as suddenly—his hands snatch up my own and grasp them fiercely...almost painfully. Our eyes meet again, but this time he holds his ground. I can feel him trembling and his eyes are pained and pleading. Those beautiful eyes. Now I know why he is here.

"I just needed to see you again," he says to me, very near to tears now.

I extract my hand from his vice-like grip and touch his face with my palm. My fingers stroke along the side of his ear and move up towards his temple and back. It is greying now. It is oddly tickling and comforting to feel the growth of his stubble. He makes a sound akin to half a laugh, and half a sigh. It is followed by a whimper and his hand moves to press mine against his cheek. His eyes squeeze tightly together and I move beside him to cover his head with my *sen*. Shielded from public view, Saeed begins to weep, softly, for he is a very proud man.

[Past—Japan]

「只今！」I hear from the kitchen faintly.

「あっ、お帰り！」I shout back, "Did you remember the rice?"

I wait a few seconds, but he doesn't reply. I put the lid back on the pot and set the ladle down. When I turn, I see him smiling. A sack of rice sits near him on the wooden floor. He is still in his suit—the striped one with the light coloured tie—legs slightly apart, hands behind his back. Apart from his smile, his face is very relaxed. This can only mean one thing. He is being mischievous.

「何、どうしたの？」I ask.

The corners of his mouth reach farther, curling into a broad grin.

「プレゼント持って来たんだよ」he replies sounding devious; lowering his voice.

I roll my eyes and smile suspiciously, wondering what in the world could be behind his back. Saeed always had a bit of a mischievous streak. He liked to do things to surprise me every once in a while. He said it made his heart melt when he watched me react...to see a light shine in my eyes or my face bloom to joy...these things were his nectar, and he, a chattery hummingbird, flitting to the next brightly coloured blossom. Even so, his gifts were...*interesting*. It could honestly be any-thing...matching thong underwear, a flower, a simple kiss, an elegant handkerchief. He never failed to sur-prise me.

"What is it?" I ask cautiously. His eyes begin to twinkle.

"Come a little closer, and I'll tell you," he says softly.

I move towards him and stop just out of his reach.

"Closer," he moans invitingly.

Now it is my turn to smile. I take two more steps and wait. I look up at him, raising my eyebrow.

"Well?" I ask.

"Give me a kiss, and I'll tell you," he says seduc-tively, almost whispering.

I begin to laugh, and playfully strike his shoulder.

"I know this game! You'll have me naked before you give me a thing! Do you even have anything back there?" I ask, trying to see behind his shoulders, but he moves to block me; obviously amused.

I hear a pop and turn back to the stove.

"Sheeyait!" I call out, and move to adjust the crock-ery, but Saeed grabs my wrist, preventing me.

"I still have something for you," he says, gorgeous eyes boring into my own, mischievous smile pene-trating my heart and making my knees weak. "I think you'll really like it," he continues, pulling me closer and beginning to kiss my neck softly, up and down.

"Mmmm, I'm liking *this*," I say, closing my eyes.

Even though he is wearing cologne, I detect his true scent. It drives me wild and he knows this...very often he uses it to his advantage. I can't explain why, but something about it is soothing and commanding and reassuring, and powerfully strong. He brings us closer until I am pressed against his thick chest. I can feel its firm muscle through our shirts, his powerful heart pounding boldly against my sternum.

"I've been thinking about you all day," he says kissing me, hands moving down my back. "I could not concentrate," he rumbles, hand moving lower...another kiss, "I wrote poetry for you," lower, he nuzzles his head against me tenderly, inhaling, "I could not stand for an hour," he rumbles close to my ear.

I burst out laughing, and he followed suit.

"It's true," he remarked between breaths, "and we had a department meeting!"

The image is too overwhelming for me and I break away laughing. I hear another pop and dash to the stove, where I tend to the food. Satisfied, I turn the flame off and return my attention to him. He has moved closer now, and he takes a small package from behind his back. My face lights up immediately.

「ウァ～!イカせんべい！？」I shout out, delighted. 「ありがとう！」

I wrap my arms around him and kiss his temple. I can't resist having one, and so I open the package to have a taste. Nothing is better than the taste of rice cracker and dried squid, and as I open my eyes, I catch him eyeing me. It pleased him so to see me happy. It pleased him so to do anything he could to show me he loved me.

2

[Present Day—Nepal]

We do not linger, for Saeed has more to say, though I can only guess at what it could be. I rewrap the *sen* around my shoulders and pay while Saeed sniffles and wipes at his face. We leave the restaurant, walking slowly along the gravel and dirt road…each saying nothing. The only place we can go to be alone is the monastery really—as ironic as that is—so I lead him in that direction. He is still silent, and falls slightly behind me as we reach the gate, hesitating.

"Please," I say motioning, but still he does not move.

It is then—for the first time in nearly ten years—that I grab his hand. I tug at it and after only slight resistance, he allows himself to be led into my home.

I do not release his hand once we have crossed the gate's threshold, but hold fast to it as I lead him through the courtyard. As I touch him, as I hold his hand within my own, I find it wondrous and mildly amusing to feel the beginnings of an erection. Observing the phenomenon, neither encouraging nor discouraging it, I allow it to run its natural course. Presently it begins to fade. It wasn't enough that anyone would have noticed it… at least, I assume not. That my body should respond to such a thing even after all these years is truly remarkable. Though part of me wishes to know whether he has also responded in this way, I place the thought aside.

As we approach closer to the temple, I can feel the way his body is reacting and responding to such a new and strange environment. The disciples and faithful laypeople have come for their afternoon *kora*. They will pray and circumambulate the temple, increasing their merit. I feel how stiff his step seems to be. This must all seem so foreign to him—elderly prostrating here, the clatter of large prayer wheels turning there, the flutter of colourful prayer flags, the constant spinning of handheld prayer wheels and the ever present chant of *om mani pad mae hum* upon the lips of each and every pilgrim, a song, a symphony of gratitude and faith making the very air we breathe.

The crowd will get thicker the closer we get. I smile, and as we come into view of the temple, I slow to a stop and allow him to take in its sheer magnificence. He takes a breath in wonder. The temple towers above us, blazing in the daylight in deep maroon, yellow, blue, gold and white. Slightly behind, encircling it in a C shape are the monks' quarters. To its left is the school, which is painted a simple cream colour, though its architecture is just as Tibetan as the other buildings. I gaze at his lips—slightly open in amazement—and remember what it felt like to have them placed upon my own...warm, and soft. Saeed was an excellent kisser, and he could kiss for hours and hours on end. Indeed, it was one of his favourite things to do. I smile, remembering these things now without desire. Funny how time distances us from all things.

We walk the slight incline up towards the temple, Saeed staring in wonder at the faithful, prostrating themselves upon the ground. He seems to have questions, but says nothing. We gingerly pass around them, and walk up the stairs towards the temple entrance. Instead of entering the temple itself, we move left, and around the corner, where we find another flight of narrow stairs leading up. He holds my hand as I lead him up towards the rooms above the temple. Once we reach the hall above the temple, we must move through another doorway which leads us higher. There are only a few rooms here now. Finally, we stop. Saeed takes in the view around him. From what he is able to see of the pilgrims passing below, they must seem like ants, though we are not so high. I produce the key to my room and unlock it, opening the door.

"Please come in Saeed," I say, standing to the side to let him enter.

Once inside, he stands aloof, like a stranger unsure of his path. The room is decorated modestly with one narrow wooden cot close to the floor and a traditionally patterned carpet. There is a small bookcase-slash-cupboard which doubles as a private altar. On top of this are various figures and photos of deities and lineage holders dear to me. He looks here and there—from the altar to the artistically decorated calendar on the wall to the cot to the carpet to the window and back to the altar—fidgeting oddly, eyes searching for a suitable place to sit.

I walk to the side of the bookcase and pick up the flower patterned thermos. I then produce two porcelain bowls from the cupboard and proceed to pour butter tea. I catch his eye as I turn with the tea and indicate he should sit on the cot with my chin. He sits. I hand him his tea and sit down cross-legged beside him. Having him this close to me—on a bed no less—after all these years is strangely odd and refreshing, but he looks so sad. I sip at my tea. Saeed tastes his and then sets it aside. His brow twists into a frown. The weight of his unspoken words threatens to crush him and I smile, remembering for all his bravado he is a delicate and gentle man. I set my own tea down and then reach out to touch his face, sighing inwardly at the feel of his skin—a gesture so familiar and yet distant, far removed. I draw him closer to me and embrace him, kissing the top of his head and giving that which was so needed. His head rests against my chest and he nuzzles closer towards my armpit. Presently our bodies reverberate with his sobs and I feel the wetness of his tears. I stroke his head and rub his back, but he still weeps. It escapes before I notice it really, but I hear the sound of my voice murmuring in Farsi.

"My poor Saeed," I whisper, "What has happened?"

He begins so low that at first I must strain to hear him, but soon I begin to recognize the pitch and tone of his voice and follow along.

"My father is dead." He says the last word hoarsely and swallows before continuing. "It happened three months ago, after so much pain and such a long, long fight." He takes another breath, and releases it with a heavy sigh. "Our last discussion was about you." As he says this, his voice changes pitch and becomes softer. He pauses a moment to compose himself. I arch a single eyebrow, but remain silent. "He knew," Saeed says shakily, "He must have known. For how long, I don't know. But earlier in the morning, when I helped him bathe, he asked after you. 'How is your friend in Japan?' he asked, 'His letters have stopped coming'".

I felt my heart begin to beat faster. Saeed had never told his parents we were together—understandably so, for he could never be sure how they would react. I never pressured him on the issue, for I knew firsthand the result of announcing surprising news to family members. It proved interesting that I had the not so pleasant opportunity to experience this again when I announced I would be ordained. But Saeed always seemed loathe to speak of his family—almost as if he were ashamed.

"I told him you lived in Nepal now and that you had become a monk," Saeed continued softly, " 'Ah, and so he does Allah's work now' he said, and he smiled, pausing before continuing. 'And perhaps this is why the letters do not come. It is the will of Allah you know, all is the will of Allah. I lie here dying, but I tell you I am not sad, for I know it is the will of Allah. Your friend has given his life to Allah, why should you still write to him?' he asked. I told him inconsistent replies or not that I cared about you very much and that we had been close. 'You must have been very close.' He said to me softly."

I frowned. What purpose did telling me this tale now serve?

Saeed continued, "Three years earlier we quarreled about you—or more specifically, my writing letters to you. He accused me of spending too much time writing and receiving letters, telling me to look at myself, and questioning why I should seem as if my entire world had collapsed when I failed to receive one. 'You worry too much for these letters' he told me, 'One letter and your face shines as if it's known no higher joy. A month without one and you look as if death itself had visited our home. Tell me, have you not everything your heart could desire? What of your wife?' he asked, 'your beautiful child?'"

I felt my heart stop. "You have a child?" I asked softly.

Saeed paused and looked up towards my face. I refused to meet his gaze. I knew Saeed had taken a wife. I will never forget the day I found out, but—perhaps foolishly—I did not expect that he would have had a child.

"A daughter," he said softly.

I find my emotions mixed. For Saeed to be a father in and of itself is neither good nor bad. Yet, I cannot deny some part of me is wounded with this revelation. When did it happen? And with all the letters we had sent, why did he not tell me? I think. If they had quarreled about this three years earlier…well, yes, I suppose I had ceased returning his letters by then—I had long since stopped reading them. It was too painful.

Saeed waits some time before continuing, "I thought it strange, but all that time he must have known… he must've…" he says trailing off, lost in memory. I gently rub his back and bring him back to the present. His voice takes on a dark quality as he speaks his next words. "He died after evening prayer, that same day he asked why I still wrote to you.

That afternoon," Saeed said, sounding darker with each word. "He became very peaceful. His pain seemed diminished. Right before lunch, he asked to speak with each of his family members. So many of us had assembled. We knew he was close to death.

When he asked to see me, he looked at me hard. This was not the gaze of the father I had known, do you understand? Something was different. 'You will burn in Hell,' he said to me, nearly spitting the words at me. Never have I seen such hate in a man's eyes. I don't know why, but instead of getting angry, I told him the truth. I'm already there, I told him. I've watched these years as this disease has destroyed your body, watched all the pain it put you through, and I've been able to do nothing. I experience this pain each night, sharing my bed with a woman who has become my wife—a woman I can never truly love. I feel it each time I look into the face of our daughter because I know that she has been born of a lie." Saeed paused and took a ragged breath. "He wouldn't even look at me after that," he continued, voice wavering, " 'Get out' he told me. Those were the last words he ever said to me."

I hold to him tightly now, for I understand he has been through so much pain, but there is more to his story, and he begins to speak again.

"The first month after my father's burial was uneventful. But then one morning as my mother was preparing breakfast in the kitchen, I found she would not face me. 'Is it true?' she asked suddenly. I had no idea what she was talking about of course, but when I asked her, she only gripped the edge of the sink tighter. 'Before your father died,' she told me, trailing off…she couldn't even finish her thought. What was I supposed to tell her? Apparently my silence was enough to convince them. For soon I heard the sound of soft sobs behind me. I turned to see my wife weeping. She had been listening. And I think on that day, that day that he bade each of us farewell, perhaps he told her as well."

He pauses again, and then sits back and looks at me. "I lied to them. I lied and told them that I needed time to think; that the grief was still too near to me and that I needed to be alone so I could clear my cluttered thoughts, but the truth is," Saeed's voice trembled, and he took my hands within his own. "The truth is, only you exist there." I feel my breath catch in my throat. "And you exist there," Saeed continues, "because I still love you."

My world stops and I am frozen in time, thought, word, and deed. To hear him say these words to me in Farsi makes my heart flutter because it is the only language which will reveal his inner-most depths through its words. In this language I can hear the weight of the agony he has gone through. I can feel the weight of the decision to seek me out—even though I stopped corresponding with him—and feel exactly how deep and true he is to his word when he claims to love me.

"I know it has perhaps become too late," he continues, almost pleading, "but please tell me you can love me as you once did."

His hand reaches up and traces the line along my chin. I take it in my own and kiss it, closing my eyes.

"Oh Saeed," I sigh.

Somewhere in my heart I want to shout. I want to scream. To love is such a simple thing. To love this man comes easily and is very natural to me. But I left him long ago, donned new robes, and took a new path. How is it that our paths diverged only to intersect again here and now…in this place? How can I begin to answer him, and what would I say if I could? These are the questions which race through my mind as his eager and far too innocent, but beautiful eyes gaze into my own. Yes, it seems a simple thing to love this man, but it is not. Nor will it be until we know exactly what our love would mean.

In all honesty, there is nothing more I would have liked to do at that moment, than throw my head back and laugh. It wasn't really the type of thing to laugh at, but what choice was I left with really? What was I possibly supposed to say to him? I wanted to laugh… laugh for all the fools in all the world who had dared to give up love…laugh for the cruel tricks time plays by wheedling through your heart and making you long for something which has long since ceased to exist… yes, laugh… I wanted to laugh as much as I had hurt over him. I could try to soothe and comfort him, but my words would be hollow, for I could not believe them. But I did neither of these things, instead choosing to sit and contemplate the words he had just said in stunned silence. So we sat there facing one another on my simple cot until his expression hardened.

"Aren't you going to say something?" he asks me tersely.

I wait a few minutes before I begin to speak. "What do you want me to say Saeed?" I ask wearily, not willing to begin an argument right here and now.

He frowns, and looks away. "I think you've just said it," he replies somewhat sullenly.

"Saeed," I begin, trying to smooth things over, but

he holds his hand up to silence me and stands, crossing to the other side of the room.

"I am such a fool," he mutters to himself.

"No, no, you're not a fool," I say softly, looking down at the blankets.

Saeed whirls to face me, eyes round and piercing with anger...shock...hurt. Though I know it will be very hard for him to hear, I must tell him.

"Saeed, if this were just between the two of us, then...well, maybe there could be a chance for things to be different, but I've taken my final vows already. I have promised myself before the Buddha, the Dharma, and the Sangha."

I hope that somehow this explanation has meaning to him, for he has never been a religious man. Saeed is silent for a stretch before replying.

"You made a promise to me too once," he spoke slowly, reaching into his pocket. "I was a fool then, for I did not understand how such a fragile, beautiful promise must be kept." He takes his fist from his pocket and stretches it out towards me, moving closer. "But I have come to realize my responsibility. I know it is late. I know. But please, please tell me somehow we can work things out. There must be some way to undo what has been done."

He lowers himself to his knees and opens his clenched fingers. My breath catches in my throat. There resting in his palm is the peach coloured ring I gave him all those years ago, when I promised I would love him forever.

3

[Past—Sea of Japan Coastline]

The wind is gentle here, and the sunlight warm. I stretch my body and feel the very essence of the ocean enter my lungs through my inhalation. Saeed rounds the corner and comes trudging up the hill. He looks cute in his beachwear—a light cotton button-up shirt and floral patterned trunks. He's removed his sunglasses, and placed them on his shirt...right where he's left it open, and the alluring forest of his chest hair is exposed to the world.

「I think there's a good spot over here,」 I say, motioning.

I see his eyes follow towards the spot I've indicated and he nods. I slip off my backpack and squat. Before long, it is open and we have fetched our beach sheet. He helps me unfold and place it. I add a few weights on the corners—though I doubt we'll need them as gentle as the wind is today—and soon we have settled in the middle; leaning against one another as we watch the waves come in.

It's nice to have a day off, and it's nice to be doing something like this together. Because we've come in the middle of the week, during a normal day, we have the whole beach practically to ourselves. We swim, we play, we eat the lunch we packed, and we lie together in the sun. We speak of nothing in particular, and we speak of our grandest hopes and dreams. By the time the light on the horizon turns to pink and orange, we are both satisfied and spent. We don't discuss what we'll do for dinner. We don't discuss the next day's plans. We sit right there, arms wrapped 'round one another for all the world to see.

It is then that I decide to give him the ring. I do so in silence. I do so in simplicity. His hand is on my arm, and so it seems effortless to slip it from my pocket and onto his finger. At first, he seems intrigued. Then, I feel something like a soft chuckle through the muscles of his abdomen hugged tight against my back.

「What's this for?」 he asks me, head stealing in to the side, and stretching to plant a kiss on my neck.

I turn and look deeply into his gentle, beautiful eyes. 「I love you Saeed,」 I say to him simply, 「I love you, and I will love you forever.」

I hear his laughter come gently, as he rubs his head against the side of my face. 「Forever eh? Forever is a long time. What is forever to us humans?」

I chuckle in return. 「As long as there is time, as long as there is now, as long as there is tomorrow. That's what forever is to us...*mere* humans,」 I quip, with a quick kiss on his knuckle.

Saeed laughs again, and we sit in simple silence, each holding on to our own version of what in the future will be the past.

[Past—Morioka, Japan]

「ええ？！明日からってどういうこと？」 I say, shocked.

Saeed is silent as the wind brushes against the trees. "I have told you," he begins to explain, "my father wishes to meet with me and it is very important that I go to see him. You know he has been ill."

I put my lunchbox in my lap and place my chop-
sticks on top of it. "Saeed," I say, reaching out to touch
his shoulder.

He looks very pained, and says nothing for some
time. Though I have never met his family, I know
enough about them to know that despite his reluctance
to speak of them, Saeed and his father are very close. I
hear them converse for what seems like hours over the
telephone, laughing and chatting away. Over the past
year, his father was diagnosed with a type of cancer.
He seemed to be doing well at first, but his health took
a turn for the worse.

Fearing I've said too much—maybe breaching
something he'd rather not even consider—I reach out
to take his hand. He squeezes back faintly, but his gaze
is directed elsewhere...somewhere far beyond the park
where we are sitting...somewhere far beyond the cher-
ry trees and their beautiful blossoms. I didn't know
then, that he felt as if he were dying. I didn't know he
had tried so many times to tell me, but could not bring
himself to do so. I didn't know how close he was to
telling me that night, but how he refused to do so because it would ruin the picnic I planned so hard for. We
finish our dinner in silence. I suppose, since the mood
is broken, there is no point in staying.

"Shall we go home then?" I ask, cool breeze scattering soft pink petals around us.

Saeed pulls me close to him and wraps his arm
around my shoulders. "Let's sit for a while," he says to
me, still seeming far away, "I never seem to have the

time just to sit with you."

And so we sit, Saeed holding me as if he were afraid to be blown and scattered away like the blossoms littered at our feet.

[Present Day—Nepal]

"How can you say these things to me now…now of all times," I say to him through a sigh, recovering.

This seems to encourage him, for he heatedly continues, standing to his feet and moving closer.

"Because it was not until now, this very moment that I realized what the most important thing in my life is," he says.

While these are very romantic words, and perhaps even words I am very grateful to hear, I feel an old anger rising from somewhere near my stomach.

"Can you hear yourself?" I ask him, frowning, "Can you see me? Do you even know what it means to take a vow?"

He flinches—only slightly—at this remark…I think perhaps more from my tone than the actual words themselves. He seems to consider something before he speaks next.

"These are not your words," he says solemnly.

I laugh suddenly at the absurdity of the very idea.

"What?" I ask, incredulous.

"These are the words of your pain…a very deep pain, for which I am responsible," he says.

To this I make no reply. He moves closer and sinks to his knees again, facing me.

"I'm sorry," he tells me.

Somewhere in the back of my mind I know that now of all times I should look away from him, but I find that I have met his eyes and before I really even understand what is happening, I feel something moving inside. He looks to be on the verge of tears. He has apologized, and looking into his eyes now, it is as if I can see how deep his regret truly is. It only lasts a moment, but it is enough. I quickly avert my eyes, and try to move away, but he has sensed something open within my heart, and he moves to meet me, holding fast to my arms.

"I'm afraid it's too late for 'sorry' Saeed," I say curtly, but he ignores me and pulls me closer into an embrace.

"I'm sorry," he says again, "I'm sorry. I'm sorry, I'm sorry, I'm sorry."

I try to push away, but he has always been stronger than me.

"Just stop!" I cry out, "Stop it."

But he ignores me, and only tightens his embrace.

"I'm sorry, I'm sorry. I am so sorry I hurt you," he says.

And it is there, right there, those seven simple words which reverberate through me and bring me to my defeat. I am not ashamed to weep in his arms. Actually this brings me more comfort than most else these days. I am however a bit flustered that he's caught me trying to hide my true feelings.

4

Saeed is such a beautiful man. I've always thought so. What is it about the people of that part of the world which makes them so incredibly beautiful? Saeed is a thin man, and at first glance, many assume he is frail. But he is strong.

Upon closer inspection, one might begin to see the suggestion of well developed and adequately muscled shoulders, or the hint of well defined calves. But his clothing is modest, and never revealing, so you would have to look closely to see it. His hair is full and slightly curly. Dark, and soft...it smells faintly of jasmine. His eyes are large and round—yet not unnaturally so—and incredibly expressive. They are the colour of amber. His nose is decidedly Persian, but strong and well formed. His face becomes slightly sleek, elongated, and angular from jawline to butted chin, but this slight imbalance works well with him.

His body is covered with dark hair. I used to love to feel it against my skin as we laid together. And his scent is intoxicating. I have never known what it is, but this man exudes fragrance from his skin. Many times I tried to emulate it using his colognes and various types of deodorant, but he would always chuckle at me and tussle my hair playfully. "You have to find the right combination of ingredients to bring out and enhance your natural scent," he would say to me. He was always a kind man, and for that I was grateful, though to anger him would be to risk near limb and life—or so it seemed when he was angry.

Saeed tried his best to appear clean shaven, but his hair grew so fast that he was always left with a five o'clock shadow. His neck was thin and smooth, excluding the slightest hint of Adam's apple…a tiny ripple, a small point visible only at certain angles.

It drove him WILD when I stroked, kissed, nibbled, and sucked on his ears, which stuck out from his head slightly, making him seem almost comical. At first I found it strange—though I never let him in on that—but I came to enjoy giving him such great pleasure from such a simple thing. He is a very loving man… the quality of this man's love shines forth in both his platonic and romantic relationships. Or I had always known this to be the case…which is why you could imagine my shock to discover he was engaged…and then had actually married. It was the biggest shock of my life, and it nearly destroyed my sense of self. I felt so betrayed. How, I wondered, could I have let such a deceptive man into my life? And he had come in so easily.

We met on the train. I was in Tokyo visiting friends. I had decided to give them a break from entertaining me and find something to do on my own that particular night. The train was full as usual, and I had just barely been able to secure a seat. At one of the busier stations, a crowd of people got off only to be replaced a few seconds later by more. I gazed at all the different people in similar business suits. Where did they come from and where were they going, I wondered.

As I was perusing the crowd, my eyes fell on a handsome non-Japanese man. I tried not to stare, but something about him drew me in. He caught me looking once or twice, but I quickly averted my eyes. As we neared my stop, I stood to make for the door. Our eyes met again by chance, and he smiled. I was struck motionless, and I felt my heart beating madly. I gave a polite smile with a slight bow and then moved to the door. When the train stopped, I quickly exited, but something told me to turn around. As I did so, I nearly collided with him. There we stood on the platform, awkwardly looking everywhere but at each other.

Finally, he said to me in Japanese, 「Do you have time for a quick bite to eat?」 That "quick bite to eat" lasted several hours, and by the end of the night we had exchanged phone numbers. I refused to believe I had fallen in love so quickly and tortured myself waiting until the next afternoon to text message him. 「I had a great time, thanks for showing me around,」 I wrote. A few minutes later he replied with 「I look forward to seeing you again.」 I felt as if my heart would burst. For the first time in my life there was an attractive guy who was actually interested in *me*. We dated long distance briefly—a few months—before circumstances forced us together again. I had finished one job and was pursuing another, this time further south...maybe Tokyo, maybe Shizuoka. Saeed meanwhile, had secretly interviewed for and accepted a position at Iwate University. It meant he would be moving to Morioka up north, which was only about thirty minutes away from me.

When he told me the news, I was elated. We spoke about many things then, including the prospect of being able to see each other more frequently. Saeed was the one who brought it up to begin with.

"Since we'll both be in or around Morioka anyway,

why don't we just get a place together?" he asked.

At first, I didn't know how to respond. It was a major step to be sure. I mean, at the time, what did we really know about each other? But in the end, I sort of ran out of options. I didn't want to get a place somewhere in the city only to have to leave it a few months later...and if Saeed had moved all the way up north, then there was not much point in my going south. So, we began our new domestic life together in a two bedroomed apartment with a dining room and a kitchen.

5

The deep sound of a drum breaks the moment between us. I push back from his embrace and take a step away. As I briefly glance into his eyes, I see he is hurt that I have done so. *Puja* will start soon. I wipe at my eyes and then look to the window before looking back at Saeed.

"It is time for prayer," I say softly. Saeed remains silent. "You are welcome to stay here until I return," I continue, moving to retrieve my prayer book from the counter.

"When will that be?" I hear his voice ask coldly.

I raise my eyebrow at this new turn of events and wonder what has affected him so. Surely he did not expect to come here and sweep me off my feet. I have duties and obligations to attend to as a monk, and I will not neglect them for the memories of this man I once loved.

"After an hour and a half," I tell him, pretending not to notice his tone.

As I am making my way to the door, I pause. Almost as if in afterthought, I turn to face him again, but he will not meet my glance.

"I will see you soon," I say to him with all the tenderness I can muster.

Saeed does not reply. In fact, the only clue I have as to him having heard is a heavy, heavy sigh. I close my door and begin my descent to the temple. Saeed has rattled my nerves.

6

I am thankful for *puja*. Its familiar rhythms keep my thoughts anchored in the here and now, and this is something sorely needed. As we progress through the prayers and chanting, it is almost enough to make me forget that Saeed is waiting just above us in my room. As the *puja* comes to a close an hour and a half later, I feel a certain inner-heaviness as I know I must return and face him. I linger outside the temple on the steps, chatting idly with my brethren until it is time to shut the doors of the temple for the night. I know it will be time for dinner soon, and I contemplate whether to invite Saeed to eat with us here in the monastery. Then I would have the chance to introduce him to my new family, and perhaps he would understand that my life is here now. But somehow, I feel as if Saeed would be offended to have come so far to only have to share me with others.

I begin the ascent to my room slowly, each step seeming more difficult than the last. We can have our evening meal out tonight. When I open the door, he stands to his feet to greet me; an expression of surprise on his face. I wonder what it is he could be so surprised about. Perhaps he lost track of the time. Or perhaps, he imagined I would never return…just as he did all those years prior.

"What were your plans for dinner tonight Saeed?" I ask, seeming oblivious to everything happening between us.

"I—well, I actually hadn't really thought that far ahead," he stammers in reply.

"Wonderful. Then come with me," I say. "I know a place."

7

It is easier than I expect to find a taxi at this hour, and so we are spared the confined quarters of the micro-busses. The driver is a middle-aged man of good humour, who sings along gleefully to Nepali pop music from a stereo system whose heyday faded into obscurity in the 1970s. Aside from the music and the gleeful singing, our ride is mostly silent. The driver makes an odd remark or three about the nephew of one of his cousins being ordained, and how it is a pleasure to give rides to any "of the robes". I smirk at the term, for it is one which has fallen out of use of late. I wonder what Saeed must be thinking and feeling now as we dash down the roadside, passing mountain, river, and stream. I suppose the scenery in and of itself is no shock to him at all; we could very well be in Iran…if it were drier. As we round the corner—perhaps just a bit too quickly—I hear a bleat of alarm from the back seat. "Sorry, sorry!" the driver calls out. I look back to see if Saeed is alright, and am welcomed with his sheepish smile. Instinctively, I return it. I face forward again and my hand goes to my *mala*.

[Past— Northern Iran]

"I don't ever think I've seen such beautiful mountains in all my life," I say out loud.

Saeed's face breaks into a grin, and glows with pride. "We can do some climbing if you'd like. If we start now, we can get a really nice view of the lake by midday," he tells me.

I laugh lightheartedly. "No, I don't think I'm one for climbing mountains just yet. I am liking the lakeside though. It's tranquil."

I look out over the water, placid and serene against the morning light. Such a different feel than Tehran's hustle and bustle. Saeed is silent for a long time, and when I look at him, I see his smile and a familiar glint in his eye. I shake my head as I begin to chuckle.

"You are incredible," I say. His smile is infectious.

"When we get back home…." he says, smile growing even wider as we walk.

I throw my head back in laughter and give a surreptitious glance around to gauge how visible we are to the public.

"You are only going to frustrate yourself if you keep on," I reply, "you know we can't."

Suddenly he is right beside me, close enough that I am enveloped by his scent. "But there is so much we *can* do," he rumbles suggestively.

I make a wide step to the side, glancing this way and that just to make sure.

"Tell me," he continues undeterred, "tell me what you'd do to me tonight if you could."

"Saeed this isn't funny," I say, suddenly serious, "If anyone hears us, if we're reported, if—"

"Why worry," he says cutting me off. "Look where we are," he says, "waaaay out heeeeereeee!" he shouts with his arms thrown out above his head and turning full circle on his heels.

His voice carries for a measure, and then is lost among the hushed breeze flowing through leaves of the trees.

"This isn't Tehran, we're in the countryside now. We can do as we please...basically," he mutters the last part almost as if speaking to himself.

I wish I had his confidence. Or his knowledge of the locality and its customs. I don't relish the thought of being detained, questioned, or arrested...not to mention tortured or executed by the Moral Police for a moment of indiscretion. For a moment, I begin to panic. How did I ever let him talk me in to coming here?! It sounded so incredibly and amazingly beautiful when he'd described it. I thought that surely, surely it must be just as good as he described it—if not better!

Saeed didn't go back to Iran often, but this year there was a professional conference of scholars, and a colleague to whom he was indebted was to receive some accolade or another, and so—of course—he had to go. I never expected in my wildest dreams that he would invite me to go with him. It would be a few days in Tehran, and when the conference was over, we would go up north for a proper holiday. Then, I'd continue on to Turkey, and go back to Japan while he visited with his family for a week or so. On paper, it seemed like a wonderful idea. But now that we are actually here, I marvel at the situation I've placed myself in.

The country is truly beautiful, and its people are absolutely and incredibly amazing...yet...yet I am always aware of how careful I must be. I must never appear too friendly, or too familiar with Saeed. I must look at him just so. I must not stand too closely to him, or speak too tenderly to him. And above all, I must never give anyone a hint of a reason to suspect that we are anything more than friends.

We have a wonderful time by the lake, and the trip on the whole goes off without a hitch to be sure. But I am not oblivious to the immense feelings of relief that sweep through my heart once I have crossed the border into Turkey. I am able to smile again, and look people in the eye without the suspicion that my careful performance can be seen for exactly what it is. Later, as I sit far above the ground on the way back to Tokyo, I touch my hand to the window imagining Saeed reaching up to meet me from those beautiful white-capped mountains.

[Present— Nepal]

Saeed has said nothing. The rest of our ride to the lake proved uneventful—with only the clamour from passing a few lorries. I find a porter, and soon we are on a small rowboat. The island is our destination. I choose not to dwell on the most basic and obvious questions. Part of me honestly wishes to know their answers, but another part of me is finished with the entire affair. If he loved me so much…if he loved me so much, then he should have honoured that love when he had the opportunity to do so. I am glad I am facing away from him; looking out onto the lake so that he cannot see my face and its expression.

Perhaps, I venture, I am being too cruel in thinking such thoughts. He was afraid. Of that much I am certain. His father was dying and he was afraid to tell me that he had an arranged marriage waiting for him back in Iran. He had already put it off for so many years. His father's sudden turn in health was the perfect turn of events in so many ways. The university wouldn't dare refuse his request for an immediate and prolonged sabbatical once they understood he would have to tend his father in his final days. Once in Iran, how could he do anything but marry and allow his father one final glimpse of happiness? How could he do anything other than provide him with one final sense of peace of mind before his eternal rest? Would I have done the same?

The island is almost devoid of people; with most of the visitors having retired. Saeed follows me as I take the winding path up to the steps, and then climb step after step until we are able to see the lake spread out beneath us.

"How much further?" Saeed asks, bending over with his hands on his knees.

"We're almost there," I say, making a mental note to slow down. He is not used to the altitude here.

Norbu, the owner of the small Tibetan restaurant, rushes out to greet me the instant he sees me.

"Sherab! How've you been? It's been so long!" he calls out heartily.

He has the youthful face of a young man still, but he has seen so much.

"It has hasn't it," I remark, "Was that *Losar* that I saw you last? How is your family?"

His chest swells with pride. "Fine, fine. I think my eldest will marry soon. If that bloke she's been seeing ever gets the courage to propose that is," he says with a chuckle.

I echo his laughter as Saeed's clunking footfall announces his arrival.

"This is a friend of mine from Japan," I say to Norbu, "I thought I'd bring him here and give him some amazing Tibetan food to go along with the amazing view."

Norbu bursts out into a hearty laugh, clapping my shoulder.

"We'll see what we can do. Come, come in and sit," he says with sweeping motions of his arms.

Then he switches into English and begins to tell Saeed more than he would ever want to know about the area, the restaurant, and of course, the food.

8

[Past— Japan]

I hadn't really expected to get anything, but I checked the mailbox as an afterthought. At first, I was surprised. Then I felt myself begin to smile. Our letters must have just missed each other. I was out later than I expected and half debating whether or not to eat out or go on home. Walking around downtown didn't present me with any appealing options, and so I made my way to my usual bus stop. After the bus came and I was on board, I decided to get off a few stops early and swing by the supermarket. I could pick up some croquettes, and maybe find some discounted sushi. I had been in the house and was just about ready to sit down to eat before checking the mail suddenly popped into my head. And when I checked, there it was. A letter from Saeed.

Though he'd been gone nearly a year, we were in regular contact with each other. Though he called occasionally, we both preferred writing to each other so much more. If I'd been a little more patient, perhaps I'd have noticed how marred the writing was…almost as if written in haste. As I closed and locked the door, I found myself ripping the letter open, eager to read Saeed's news. But as my eyes scanned over the words on the page, I felt my blood run cold.

I am not returning. By the time this letter reaches you, the ceremonies will have been completed, and I will have been wed to the woman who is to be my wife. How can I tell you how this has happened? God how I wanted to tell you. God how I tried to tell you. I am sorry. I do love you. I am sorry.

Saeed

There were no greetings, no pleasantries, no long, poetic verses describing the scenery as he biked to and from his errands for his mother. Just these simple words.

[Present— Nepal]

"This is really amazing," Saeed says between another bite of his *momo*s.

I smile. "I'm glad you like them. I'm sure Norbu will be pleased as well," I reply.

Saeed flashes me a smile, and part of me feels as if my heart will burst.

"Do you think he'd be willing to part with the recipe?" he asks.

I laugh. "Somehow I sincerely doubt it," I remark, "but you can always try."

Saeed chuckles for a moment before we fall into a comfortable silence.

"This is nice," he says finally, eyes gazing into his plate.

I turn to look at the lake below and the scene stretched out before us. "It is," I say, "I was hoping you'd enjoy it."

"No," Saeed counters, he seems amused, "I meant us. This. This is nice...being here...with you."

His eyes slowly lift to find mine, and we are suspended in an infinite moment of silence and possibilities. The type of silence where love is a beautiful destination of crystalline light, and the world and all its noises have faded like yesterday's sunsets.

"My daughter would love you," he says softly.

My eyebrow rises along with my heartbeat.

"Would she now? How old is she?" I ask.

Saeed's grin breaks into a full-blown row of immaculately white teeth. "She's just turned four," he says. "God I wish I could have brought her with me. She would love it here. And you would love her. She is so…so full of *life*. It's amazing."

I maintain the façade of pleasure on my face, but I am thinking that this man must be mad…absolutely mad. He has a daughter…that he would bring with him…*here*? To what end? To convince me that we could be a family?

"I know it's so cliché, and I thought it was too until I actually became a father, but they…they change your whole life…y'know?" he says to me.

No, I think back at him. *No I do not know Saeed. Tell me exactly how it is that they change you. Do you understand what loyalty is now? Honesty? Do you understand the meaning of what it is to have a duty and an obligation to be straight forward enough with someone to tell them that you are leaving their life and will never see them again? Do they teach you how to truly love?* These are the thoughts that flow through my mind as he talks about the way her face lights up each and every time he enters the room, or how she expresses the most innocent and complete joy at the simplest of tasks in her daily life. I listen politely, and I am indeed moved. But it is for a far different reason than he thinks—if he even has the capacity to know how I feel anymore.

After dinner we linger to chat with Norbu, and then begin the descent to the boats. In the fading twilight, our hands find one another, and we are once again transported to the fragile world of comfort and familiarity…a world where we can exist unannounced and unfettered for the space of a dream. But I have vowed to see through illusion and be rid of attachment. How then shall I navigate this world of dreams Saeed is so intent upon leading us towards. And how could we ever rebuild the foundation of a relationship which was so fractured and flawed to begin with—for how could it not have been for it to have lacked the transparency and openness to discuss his marriage in Iran? Marriages don't just happen. They are planned. There are dates. Milestones. Preparations. Promises…above all promises. And how would he propose that we keep promises of love between one another now?

After we have reached dry land again, I lead him to another monastery, and—still hand-in-hand—we spin the prayer wheels as we circumambulate the temple. We do so in silence. He, with a faint and besmitten smirk on his face. Who knows what fantasies are playing out in his head. For my part, I pray that he is liberated. Liberated from his attachment to me…liberated, from what he feels is his understanding of love. I truly hope that one day… one day, Saeed can be freed.

We reach home well after the monastery gates have closed for the night, but I have my key. Before I go, I walk him to his hostel, and we spend a quiet moment gazing at the stars.

"I do not think I would trade anything for this moment right now with you," he says. "Thank you."

In reply I move close to him and very gingerly give him a peck upon the cheek. "Good night Saeed," I say to him as I turn to walk away. "I'll come calling tomorrow afternoon."

I feel his eyes on me as I walk down the path towards the monastery, and only when I am safely inside of its gates can I truly breathe easily again. It was a lovely night, and I am glad to have had it, but I know I have no future with that man. And my heart is heavy with the knowledge of my obligation to convey this to him. It is quiet when I reach my room, and even quieter still as I fish out pen and paper, and begin to write my letter.

9

My Dearest Saeed,

*Thank you. Thank you for coming to see me after all these years. Truth be told, I stopped writing you all those years ago because to some extent I was still trying to heal. Please understand that I no longer hold you to any blame, but it took a very long time for me to accept that you had married. Our relationship had been so...so **right** Saeed. Our love had been so right. It was hard for me to imagine a time when there would not be love between us. I imagined that we would live out our days there in Morioka, and die happily together in one another's arms. But things have a way of turning out quite differently than we plan.*

After I heard the news of your marriage, I left Morioka. Some months later I left Japan. Where I went and what I did, I would rather not tell you—truth be told I'd rather not remember myself—but everything I did, every action, every choice I made was born of pain. I was in such a state of pain and I remember how I tried so hard with so many things to deaden it completely. It never truly worked. And one day, I woke up on a beach in Thailand next to a knife. I cut my hair and begged sanctuary at the nearest monastery but they thought I was crazy. So I searched and searched until I found one which would take me in. I remained with them three months. It would have been easy to disappear into anonymity with them there, but my visa was about to expire, and I was afraid of Thai prisons. I set out for Nepal. The first place I went in Kathmandu was Boudha. If you ever have the chance, you should go. Somehow as I turned the large prayer wheels, I gained comfort. It was as if I felt myself being freed of layer after layer of pain. I was glad to be there Saeed, and I vowed to find a way to stay forever. I inquired at several monasteries, and was secretly pleased when they led me nowhere. Though Kathmandu is truly one of the world's greatest cities, I had no desire to join a monastery there in particular.

One day I happened across a traveler…he was a refugee in fact I think, but at the time I did not know it. He told me of this monastery here, not too far from Pokhara, and to my heart something sounded right. I set out for it the next day and, when I got here, joined the monks in prayer. The abbot was not in the least bit surprised when I asked to join. Of course there were conditions to be fulfilled and a novitiate period, but they accepted me with open arms. Though I never forgot about you or the love we shared, the memories became less painful. Over the years, they became things I cherished, and I was able to release the pain. In truth I had not thought about you for a very long time until I received your message the other day.

I was glad to see you Saeed, to tell you anything else would be a lie—and I refuse to tell them to you here… there have been too many between us. You are still the same strong, and proud and handsome—oh yes, still very handsome Saeed—man I fell in love with all those years ago and spending time with you this brief time I felt the stirrings of such emotions on the edge of my heart. You have always been so brave Saeed. It took great courage to come here and reveal the deepest feelings you had kept locked within your heart. I know how difficult it must have been for you to admit this Saeed. But I am afraid I must be the bearer of sorrowful news.

Saeed I have been ordained, and I shall remain a monk until I am liberated and leave this world far behind. What is love Saeed? What is love? Do you remember the Ainu song I used to sing...the song about being a bird and flying to my love? I feel it speaks to our current state of affairs, but which of us has become the bird, and which of us is unable to speak? If I were to tell you that I did indeed still love you, it would hold little meaning for you. This would be so because we could never touch each other in the same way again. You are a great many things Saeed, but celibate is not one of them. Your sexuality must be embraced and expressed in a very basic physical and natural way. You require this nourishment as a plant requires water. It is grossly unfair to ask you to do without it, for ultimately it would do you great harm. And as much as I love you, I will not break my vows.

I think about you and the way our bodies rubbed against each other. I feel the heat of your flesh against mine moving, writhing beneath my skin as if your very lifeblood had awakened and eaten its portrait across my chest. I weep for the life we had. I weep for the love we shared. But we cannot return. Saeed, you must return home. You must return home and be a father to the daughter that you've helped create. She is the innocent one, and to leave her now would only teach her to hate.

Saeed please, there is too much hate in this world already. We must not allow our selfish actions to create more. It would be best if you never came here again, for I fear our meeting would only ever leave you—and my heart—in the fiercest of pain. Do you understand why I ask you to do this Saeed?

Do you understand why I need to know that you are home safe with her? It is so I can be here with my brothers, and lead a life unfettered and free of delusion. I have long understood exactly who and what I am, and what I am cannot be concealed behind closed doors and the watchful eyes of the moral police. Neither shall I allow the guise of "friendship" to be the chador for our love. Though it hurts me to say so now, I can never bloom and come to fruition with you Saeed...we both know this. We must stop pretending. I will always love you. But the love that we shared will never again have the same shape, or meaning. You deserve someone who can give of themselves entirely unto you...and this I cannot do.

Know that my prayers will always be with you Saeed...with you, and your family. You have a chance to love and be happy. Do so. I know you are not a religious man Saeed, but please accept the rosary I have sent with this letter. This was the first rosary I ever owned as a monk, and I would like you to keep it in memory of me. I do hope one day, perhaps in some other life, you will come to understand it is because of love that I have released you. Spread your wings and fly home. You are free Saeed, I release you. Please take care.

With All My Love,

Sherab Gyatso

10

I knew these words would wound him. I knew these words would wound him beyond measure, but at the same time I knew I had to say them. If not for myself, then for his daughter...and mother...and wife. Yes, most of all she...she who had only loved and expected to be loved in return. How could I ask her to relinquish her love? What could I say to make her understand my selfish desires? How could I justify inflicting such sorrow—a direct result of my own joy? No, robes or no robes, I will never find joy as a direct result of another's pain. I refuse to do so.

The next morning, I feel the sun rise as we pray. I keep the letter in my shirt pocket; closest to my heart. I wait until the afternoon, when we have our free time, before calling out to one of the younger monks going into town. He approaches me curiously as I remove the letter from my pocket and bring it to my lips.

I am no longer in the monastery when the letter is delivered to Saeed. I am watching silently from the hostel down the road. I know when he has read it...how I cannot explain through methods most will understand, but I know. I can feel it. And somewhere far away I hear the sound of anger drowned in sorrow. Hopefully...very hopefully this anger will not transform itself—or its owner—into hate.

Saeed leaves our settlement dejected and alone. His head cast down, his eyes red and wet. Wrapped 'round his left wrist is my rosary. All decisions have consequences.

The children run 'round him kicking their ball along, and a small herd of goats bleats as they trot past, but he cannot see them, for he is lost within his own sorrow—a sorrow of his own creation. I watch until he is but a tiny speck against the landscape, and suddenly he turns in my direction and looks up. He is very still. I tense, fearing that he has somehow become aware of my presence, but I know in my heart he does not see me...he never will again.

The bus eventually stops by the roadside and he boards it. It tinkers to life and rumbles away, carrying him, and all his hope of our future with it. The sun will set and the moon will rise. I am not a callous man, but somehow, I am unmoved by his parting...he who always felt so free to come and leave as he saw fit.

The next day I rise, and all is as it should be within my world. The drum sings softly and we are drawn to prayer. The horinets clang and the long-horns wail their deep and soulful call. I call on Tara to assist in healing and Mahakala to assist in overcoming obstacles. Our chanting uplifts and transforms whatever thoughts I held of sorrow into deep contemplation, and compassion. Hopefully, he will return and be a father to his daughter and a husband to his wife. Hopefully, he will not cling on to the memories of our love and allow it to destroy not only his own life, but the lives of all those around him.

Three weeks later I am awakened from a dream in tears. In the dream I am doing laundry on the roof. The sun is hot and the wind is pleasantly warm. As I hang my clothes to dry, suddenly a beautiful coloured bird comes to rest upon the clothesline. I have never seen a bird of such colour and wonder what species it could be...its browns and greens and golds seeming too mute for the birds of Nepal. It sings the Ainu song to me in Farsi and my blood runs cold: *How I wish I were a bird, how I wish I were a bird, for if I were a bird, I would fly to my love. Ah but a bird cannot speak, a bird cannot speak... should I become a bird, I will lose all speech.*

I am not a bird Saeed.

It is only then, three weeks later, that I realize my heart has once again broken. I contract a fever and am sometimes very cold. Then I become quite hot and agitated, and then I vomit and cannot keep any food down. All the while, my thoughts turn to Saeed...this man I have so coldly thrown back into the world...a man alone in the world, and without love.

We are not birds. Our songs are ripped, wrenched, and strangled from our breasts. And with our broken hearts, we can no longer fly. Who will scatter seeds of joy for us now? Who will sing the songs that give us courage, and drive us to Love? Who will sow the seeds of healing and affection to soothe the wings of our aching souls? I am no bird Saeed, and you have broken my heart. I wrap these robes around the remainder of my frail body and weep. I weep each and every day through the prayers I speak to be whole again, to be healed again, to be loved again. I learn the languages of old and the mantras of eras long past in hopes of transforming and transporting my sorrow...in hopes of using it for the benefit of all beings. But what have you ever known of honest action for the benefit of others?

I am not a bird. But if I were, I fancy myself the type of bird whose song would make your cold and callous heart tremble. I fancy this bird that I would be would strike terror in the hearts of common men. The notes and melodies of my warbling would bring forth only Truth. Deception, and all that is hidden would be revealed in plain sight. My wings would be strong, my feathers silky and soft. When I alighted on your windowsill, or rested in the branches of the fig trees of your gardens, you would beg and plead for me to leave. You would leave small jeweled plates adorned with flowers, rosewater and delicious fruits in offering. "Pray be silent dearest one," you would beg, "Please be still!" For you would understand that to hear my song would mean to hear the very voice of that which is Truth, and even your feeble and foolhardy minds would understand within the Light of Truth, all that is of shadow simply cannot exist.

I would regard you as you are—simple, and unmoved. Then I would spread my glorious tailfeathers, and sing.

Sing Saeed. You are free now. Sing.

Mahamalamaya

Mahamalamaya

1

The wind dances along the edges of my skirt as I ascend the stairs. It's cold tonight and my toes feel cramped and numb in my boots. It is dark here, much darker than in the streets below.

I search for him with my eyes. Such an inefficient way of finding things, but the longer I use this vessel, the more accustomed I become to its limitations. He is here, very close now. I can feel him. A small flicker of reddish light betrays his presence. I step onto the roof, slowly approaching. In the darkness he leans against the water tower almost nonchalantly. As he exhales, a plume of acrid smoke mixed with vapor trails upwards...slowly, gently. He leans his head against the tower and sighs a deep sigh. He is aware of my presence, of that I am certain, though he does not acknowledge it.

As my senses adjust, I examine him more carefully. He is a handsome man, face framed with layered hair falling just below his chin at its longest point. Though his build is only slightly better than average, I feel certain he would have no problem holding his own. He has inquisitive eyes, lighter than the color of his eyebrows, which somehow makes them stand out. He is one who knows how to use his charm, and he is also intelligent, but dangerously so. His is the type which always seeks to push the limits and test the boundaries. He likes a good mystery, and he feels stagnated and bored with the offers of ordinary life. He is far too young to understand the consequences of summoning such evil. It is ironic that one who seems so innocent should be the cause of such a disturbance. As my eyes scale up and down this figure, I address him.

"You?" The word escapes sounding surprised. "You summoned that creature."

His reply comes slowly. "It's getting closer each time…I—I think It's looking for me."

"Of course It's looking for you," I snap, agitated, "and rest assured It will find you. Did you plan to run forever?"

He looks off to the side, flustered. "I just—I just need some time to figure out what to do," he says sheepishly.

"Well time is not on your side," I snap back, "we need to get you somewhere safe."

He turns his face towards me questioningly. "Safe?" he echoes back stupidly.

"Somewhere away from other people," I reply.

"Who are you?" he asks still looking confused.

"We have more important issues to deal with now," I say ignoring him; beginning to walk away.

I hear his voice coming from behind me, hesitant and uncertain. "Is It…is It really evil?" I whirl around and fix him with a hard stare. He begins to shrink in upon himself.

"You are an idiot," I spit at him, making him wither like a dried out weed.

As I begin to walk again, I hear his small voice. "I-I wasn't trying...."

He follows behind me like a puppy that's been scolded, yet is too stupid to believe it is unloved. My steps are quick and determined. My boots rap their angry rhythm on the pavement. This creature grows more powerful by the hour and the bind I have placed on It will not hinder It long, I fear. Before It is able to see—feel—him again, I must place him within my own protection; rendering him effectively invisible. To his credit, as we walk, he offers no explanations for his actions. There are no excuses or piteous apologies, no attempts to sway my sympathy. He seems surprised as I walk directly to the door of his apartment. He lingers further behind me now and eyes me strangely. I can feel his heartbeat quicken.

"Who are you?" he asks me again, hesitantly.

I position my back to block his view as my hand swings upward to meet the doorknob. The sound of locks clicking echoes oddly to his ears in this lonely, dim hallway. It must seem so loud to him. The door swings open to reveal blackness.

"Won't you come in?" I say patronizingly, stepping off to the side.

For a moment, there is no sound except his shallow breathing, breath which quivers and mirrors the look of terror in his wide eyes. I regard the look on his face. He looks as if he's about to soil his pants.

"I'm becoming impatient," I tell him, looking into his eyes.

Now he begins to shrink into his sweatshirt and his mouth begins to quiver. He walks into the apartment. It smells old and musty here despite the recently polished wooden floor...some lemon based polish perhaps. I shut the door behind me, and hear the sound of a match striking. He lights several candles. Perhaps this comforts him. His fear seems to have diminished, though it still remains. I feel it thick around him...in layers and sheaths, though carefully guarded. He understands he may have to use it.

I scowl in semi darkness. His type are the worst, always seeking that which they can use to their benefit. Even now I feel his curiosity about me and what he can coax from me.

The apartment seems very spacious...in part due to the high ceilings. There is no furniture here, only stacks upon stacks, rows upon rows of yellowed papers—charts?—and books which are older than this city. The stacks are haphazard and slovenly. They lean against the walls forming a boundary of some sorts. It is their collective countenance which provides the odor.

It is only when I step closer do I notice the markings on the floor. At first glance it appears to be a mandala made of white chalk. Upon closer inspection I see many different mantras, written mainly in Sanskrit, though I detect a smattering of Pali. One other script catches my eye. You see it on the Tibetan temples, for it is the script upon which theirs is based. For this writing—largely unknown and forgotten—to be here in this way is a cause for great alarm.

The mandala has been deactivated, this much is immediately apparent, but the energy that has been released from it has left its impression, an aura, for all those who are able to detect it. He watches off to the side like a curious rat...waiting to see how I move, waiting to see what I do. I do not like this one. He is moving, gathering, rustling and mumbling as he sifts through pile after pile.

The mandala of mantras is strange...not merely because of its contents, but because it is incomplete. As I circle it, reading, I begin to frown. It becomes apparent that the situation—and by extension he—is much more dangerous than I had previously imagined, for none of these mantras in and of themselves are proper to the calling and raising of the creature. I begin to scan bits of them together, numerous combinations and extractions fit and gather through my mind in calculation. But still, something is amiss. None of these are right.

"What were you trying to do here," I say squatting nearer, reading more, trying to form a better picture of the situation.

His answer is a torrid flurry of confused ramblings.

"I need to get somewhere higher. It's all about the energy," he began.

One minute he was talking about humanity, and the next he dove headlong into the birth of stars. Was he even sure himself what he was talking about? As I read more, I nod. Stars, higher planes...these seem to be repeating themes. This part at least makes sense. I frown. There are smeared and broken parts of the mandala.

"What's this here?" I ask pointing.

He nears and remains silent. I glare at him. Though

the light is dim, I can still detect the look of uncertainty in his face. He swallows and clears his throat.

"Ka...ka-va, m—ma? S-s-s—aw cripes that one was sh-s—" he stumbles along.

"You can't read these," I break in, growling angrily.

With my inner eye I receive flashes of two people—another man. "Who worked with you?!" I demand.

He begins to shrink away from me as I stand. Again, he is astonished at my ability to know more than what is presented to me.

"Take me to him," I say very evenly, heading towards the door without waiting for a response.

We walk perhaps twenty minutes. It has become wet again with mist and drizzle, though still not a true rain. I follow him, scowling at his back. Stupid, I shout at him in my head. How stupid and utterly irresponsible he is. He does not understand that his actions have enabled the very foundations of his plane of existence to be altered. Hopefully, this ignorance also extends to the creature he summoned. If It were to somehow come to understand that It could alter things according to Its own designs.... I scowl harder, choosing to place the thought aside for now. I must neutralize It. And in order to do this, I must understand exactly what he's done... and how he did it.

We begin to move slowly uphill. As we climb further, a maroon colored apartment building stands out from the rest because of the angle at which it rests on a fork in the road. Instead of a corner, the end facing us is rounded with windows. The building itself does not seem too old, and it is architecturally pleasing to the eye. From the top most window, a shrouded figure seems to watch our approach, diminishing into shadow as we near...a vague shadow against darkness. He has moved his head upwards, apparently at this person. Was he sending a signal? As the figure withdraws, he looks quickly behind him to see if I have witnessed this exchange. He holds the door for me as we enter the building...how sweet.

Once inside he moves towards the lift, then, with some hesitation he changes directions towards the stairs. I can only think of two reasons for this: either he is planning to run—a foolish notion—or he is trying to buy some time for his partner. I follow, silently scowling. We climb flight after flight of stairs. When we reach the top, he glances tentatively to the side to see if I still follow, then moves into the corridor.

The carpet here matches the color of the building's exterior. He makes a bee line for the door at the far end of the hallway. Even before we reach it come the sounds of metal clicking and unlocking. He stops and raps twice upon the door. It is old and wooden...polished a deep maroon. It opens and he immediately steps in as if he lived there, speaking.

"I've bought someone to see you," he says a bit sarcastically, but somehow I still sense his attempt to show that he is in control of the situation.

In the darkness, standing partly behind the door, is a man. He gives no reply, simply a slight nod of his head. I stand in the entranceway examining this being. There is definite sadness here. It exists within this place, as well as within the heart of the man before me. He seems enveloped with it. He is a beautiful man, though somewhat frail. He has brown skin and long, straight fingernails. His hair is long and black, and braided, though a purple scarf loosely covers the top of his head. He does not meet my eyes, nor seem particularly concerned there is another person in his midst. On his face is written an expression of marked loneliness and despair, as if each breath carried sorrow and darkness with it. He holds himself as if he is afraid to move, or as if the pain of movement would crush his body and scatter his precious insides like sand swirling in a sea storm.

I immediately understand, and stepping closer, I speak directly to him. "He does not love you. You deserve better than this," I say…an accusation more than a statement.

His face betrays no sign of having heard, yet angles upwards slowly towards me.

"Have you really come so far only to tell me what I already know?" he says softly, almost as if he were amused.

I narrow my eyes at him decisively, and step into the room. He closes the door behind me, enshrouding us in total blackness. Nevertheless, he moves with ease past me and in to what I assume to be the living room.

As my eyes adjust, I can see that the other already has his coat off and is lounging on the couch with his feet crossed up on the table. His nonchalant assurance of himself angers me deeply and I feel the change happening.

"Stand to your feet you arrogant son-of-a-bitch and

take responsibility for what you've done." I say loudly.

The words come darkly, perhaps too much so, as by the time I've finished, my voice has become unnaturally deeper and my eyes are burning. Though he is doubtful, wondering whether his eyes are playing tricks on him in the dark, he senses and sees the transformation beginning and fearfully stands; slowly distancing himself from me physically. His lover—or rather the tool he has manipulated with the guise of love—has also noticed, but draws nearer.

"I think I've been expecting you," he says softly, almost hesitantly…confused, "though not in this form."

My anger still has not dissipated, and I turn towards him.

"You also," I spit, "do not think you will escape the price of your actions."

He either does not care, or is unafraid, for he steps closer still; for the first time making eye contact and somehow becoming more alive.

"But you've come about the mandala and you know time is short," he says simply as if catching a child red handed at some naughty prank.

Though I am still angry, I am intrigued, and I begin to regard him in a new light. Yes, this one is honorable, if not misguided. This much is apparent to me now.

"We will have tea," he calls out to The Coward who until now was sulking against the wall behind him, trying to hide.

Though he seems slightly reluctant, he moves into

the kitchen, fumbling in the dark before finding a light switch. I hear sounds of water filling a container, and then the sound of the stove lighting.

In the scant light that comes in from the kitchen, I am able to examine more of this apartment. The kitchen itself is painted a warm shade of yellow, darkened towards the ceiling from hours of cooking. All of the cabinets have sections of glass enabling one to see their contents. The towels and potholders are all various shades of red.

On the counter I see a row of what I assume to be cookbooks. Yes, despite all that has happened, I am left with the sense that cooking still brings this man joy. The living room is large, but full. In the light, I notice the bookshelves—all wooden—loaded with volumes upon volumes of books. Though I'd have to look closer to be certain, I'd say many were scholarly works indicative of an advanced, scholarly degree. There are two or three works of art hanging on the walls, though I'd need more light to tell exactly what they are. The curtains, the same yellow as the kitchen, are drawn shut. The couches are a mixed shade of brown and maroon. He enjoys surrounding himself in these earthy colors, a sign of his balance.

"We have no time for tea," I say, surprised at the gentleness directed towards him.

He smiles. "But you cannot act until you know exactly what was done. And while I am telling you, we will have tea," he finishes.

I should be frustrated. I should demand what I wish to know from him and shatter his China cups. But instead, I wait. Perhaps patience does have its rewards.

He sits down on one of the couches, and motions for me to do likewise. I take the one facing him, and hear the sounds of The Idiot fumbling with something in the kitchen behind me. He takes a deep breath.

"Something's come through, hasn't it," he says.

When he says this, it is very clear that he is not asking a question...almost as if the proof of something he'd suspected all along has come rapping on his front door.

"I don't know how much you already know, but that was never the intention," he continues, squinting as if remembering a bitter taste.

He stares somewhere far off, not exactly looking at me, but then again, not focused on anything in particular in the room.

"This much he's probably told you," he continues, sounding apologetic.

"No," I counter, "I am interested in hearing all you have to say."

He pauses as if considering something, then nods.

"The mandala was only to help Eath move on— reach a higher plane of existence."

I think back to references of other worlds within the mandala and nod my head.

"He mentioned something of a star," I say thoughtfully.

"Yes," this man replies, almost excited, "a star,

some new form for this body…this is what he is trying to gain, a higher form, a better vantage point, a—"

"For what purpose?" I demand, breaking in.

His reply is wrapped in sorrow, so much sorrow.

"That I've never known," he says softly.

He is gazing downwards again, lost somewhere between shadowed dreams and illusions. In my mind's eye I see images of them together, but something is not as it should be. Something horridly wrong has happened to this man. Before I can delve further, I am struck by the change of temperature. There seems to be a cool breeze coming from somewhere behind me, and the sounds of the city seem louder. I am just beginning to register the significance of this event when a squealing, high-pitched sound breaks our silence: the kettle. I leap to my feet and look behind me into the kitchen. The Coward is nowhere to be found.

"He is gone!" I shout, whirling around again to glare at this man who still gazes somewhere far away.

"He climbed out the window and used the ledge to get to the roof," he says softly, almost ashamed it seems. "From there he used the fire escape. He'll not have gotten far."

So they were in cahoots. All this time he was only creating a diversion. With these thoughts, I feel the transformation beginning again; this time stronger, more precise.

"It is within my power to destroy you," I say to him, focusing completely on him.

Though I am sure he can feel it—indeed his skin should be blistering—he remains decisively unconcerned.

"Surely you knew he would run," he begins with half an exasperated laugh. "He's always run," he finishes in a tight whisper.

Though he seems quite detached, closer inspection reveals tears trailing down the sides of his face…hollow, empty, and without emotion, though born of it. Why should I care? Why should the life of this human carry importance to me or my task? Why should I come to care about him? These things pass through my mind as I watch him weep, an eerie, heart-wrenching sight of smooth, non-emotive expression. Dead trails of water from zombie lids. I do not know the answer to these questions, yet they—he—has disarmed me and I do not wish to hurt him anymore. As I make my way towards the door, he speaks.

"I will deal with the kettle, but please turn out the light before you leave."

I gaze towards the kitchen and the apartment returns to darkness, as it was when we arrived. I become suddenly still with the coming of realization. This man is blind. As if he hears my thoughts, I hear a word uttered softly in the darkness like a sigh.

"Sometimes."

I leave this apartment with the humbling awareness that in this form even I cannot see all there is to see.

I don't know where he's going. I don't know what he hopes to gain by running, but the Blind Man is correct: he will not get far.

His trail is easy to follow, and I find the rhythmic clip-clap of my boots growing faster in anticipation...a cadence of pursuit. He doesn't even try to hide himself. He knows this is futile, and he is not so foolish as to return to his apartment...no, he already has all he needs from there. I focus on his fear. I feel it thick and cold and soft, like cream. It floats throughout the air and sticks itself, corroded, on the ground. It is rancid and smears the windows with its scent. The wind sends it towards me, wafting in bursts of frigid gusts.

Smirking, I entertain the thought of what would happen if I allow the creature to have him. He should leave the city, this much is apparent, but something about his character tells me he will not...on his own. What is he hiding? Rather, whom is he protecting? I suddenly stand still and close my eyes, listening, centering.

The external noises fade away and the image of a bookstore appears before me. In my mind's eye I move closer, and enter. Wooden floors, dust, and the smell of damp mold...an older man, balding, with owl-eyed glasses, sharp nose.... I frown and move closer. Brown, leather book, it must—my eyes snap open and I stumble forward. The force of something very near to snapping is brought to my attention. The creature is very near to breaking my bind...and It is angry. I sigh in perturbed frustration. The bookstore and the old man are important, yet at this moment I must subdue that wretched coward. I no longer have time to chase him, so I step into an alley and away from the public eye. When I am comfortably enshrouded in shadow, I disappear.

He has that disgustingly smug smirk on his face as he speed-walks along the sidewalks, only barely avoiding collision with normal day to day pedestrians…pedestrians who don't even realize the criminal amongst them. He would slaughter them all for his needs and do they even realize? Would you reading this now recognize those who walk among you in silence, concealing who they really are behind flesh and fear and bone?

He does not see me; neither is he aware of my presence. He hurries. He is heading towards the bookstore. Curious. Now more than ever am I tempted to follow him in this way, disregarding the very real danger I feel growing. Leaving things as they are, the creature will free Itself very shortly. I should let It have him. I should materialize before him and let him know I have the power to stop It but choose not to. I should do these things, and it is within my power to do them, yet despite my personal feelings I have my duty…and I will not break my vows. That is my choice.

He does not notice the sudden thickening of shadow in the corner ahead of him, where two buildings meet. He suspects naught as he begins to walk past, but suddenly finds his wrist seized; his body yanked. He has no time to scream. He hasn't time for anything really because before he can react, he sees shadow. And just as suddenly, he is released and goes tumbling down onto a dark, wet field.

"Ow!" he complains as he hits, then begins to roll.

He is confused and very afraid. This fear turns to raw panic as he lifts his head and takes in his surroundings, for he is in the middle of a field, surrounded by forest and the night of the countryside. He comes to his hands and knees and is trembling. I wait a moment for him to see me before I act. As he recognizes me, he half screams. Speaking the appropriate words, I wave my hand in his direction. His shriek is odd, a full two octaves higher than I'd expected. He rolls upon the ground, palms covering the area from his forehead to his cheekbones.

"My eyes! My eyes!" he screams over and over, and then, "help!" in increasingly higher octaves.

I would like to savor the moment of his undoing, complete as he begins to soil himself in fear (this is a first for me), but there are things to do. I focus and begin the proper chant. My words come quickly and deeply. I begin to walk around him—counterclockwise. This is unusual, though important, as I wish to bind him to the earth, here in this place.

His screams grow quieter and he begins to listen. Clever. I complete the circumference the third and final time and finish. As I utter the final syllable, a bluish colored ring of light encircles him. Closer inspection, by one who is able, would reveal the letterings of an ancient tongue, each symbol representing the sequence of syllables and sounds which are the mantra. Whether the fool I have placed here will be able to distinguish actual letters, or merely detect a ring of light I do not know…nor is it my concern. He will not be able to read it; indeed, none on this planet now retain that ability.

He waits, fearing for his life. He surprises me yet again as he does not beg for his life, or plead with me. I watch him hunched on all fours, dejected and look-ing so much like the filthy animal he is. Even now in this state his mind is whirling, calculating, devising the next move. After some time, I begin to speak.

"Though you do not realize it now, I have saved you," I say to him.

"You bitch!" he shrieks, voice cracking. "What have you done to my eyes?!"

I sigh, "Your eyes will be fine by and by".

This is true, as I only wished him blinded to the working of his bind.

"You bitch," he mutters again.

"You should be thankful," I tell him, mildly annoyed.

"Where are we?!" he interjects.

"Somewhere where you'll be safe," I tell him softly, then, "tell me about the man in the bookstore…the one with owl-eyed glasses".

He immediately stiffens, but remains silent.

"This is fine," I say nonchalantly, "I have my own methods".

I walk towards the forest, reaching the trees before turning to regard him. We are very far from the city. He is placed well here in this clearing. He will not be found.

2

I enter and allow the door to close behind me. The sound of a bell alerts my presence to the empty room. As I step down and proceed forward, the smell of old books, dust, and mold waft towards me. There are many books here, yet the vast majority are of no interest to the average person. A steady handful of scholars here and there with an ever rotating number of graduate students immersed in research, these are the typical customers of this shop. That, and those whose interests lie beyond this world. Those who seek the knowledge of the Unseen congregate here. The collective longing of their hearts splashes loudly through the room as an echo of what was and what is yet to be. They are drawn here to feed and satiate a relentless and unending hunger of that which is forbidden, though which gives of itself freely to all.

"We are closing," comes the voice of an older man from somewhere in the far back darkened corners and rooms behind the counter.

An angry thumping sound grows closer and closer pounding loudly upon the floor, and soon the man with owl-eyed glasses appears, face contorted to a frown, cane in hand. He stops short when he reaches the counter, taken aback at the new face, curious as to what I could possibly want. He wonders am I lost. He wonders am I curious. He wonders am I dangerous, and rests one hand under the counter where he keeps his old revolver.

"If there's something I can help you with, please let me know…I'm about to close the shop and call it a night," he tells me.

His manner is shrewd, his voice steely, and he has the countenance of a pedophile. His large eyes blink behind his lenses. He tilts his head, and he begins to examine the shape of my body.

"That is fine, I won't take long," I say to him, "I've

come for Eathan's book."

His eyebrows rise and his mouth makes a curious smile.

"You? How do you know Eathan?" he asks, almost mockingly.

It's obvious he doesn't believe me, though in his amusement he brings his hand away from the revolver and changes positions—all the while glaring decisively—resting his elbows on the counter and warily using one hand to support his chin.

"We have intimate relations," I say flatly.

This wipes the smile clean from his face and it is replaced with something almost akin to disgust—jealousy.

"I don't know what you're talking about," he snaps, "and anyway we're closing."

Something about the way he puts it sounds very final, and he looks at me in a very menacing way, daring me to challenge his authority. Liars…why do people feel the need to lie to me?

"You know very well which book I mean," I say meeting his glance, a glance which is very quickly turning from anger into something else…something I can't quite put my finger on. "The brown leather book with the worn strap," I continue, "the one he gave you three days ago right after he let you taste his skimpy little—"

"That's enough!" he roars out at me.

He is visibly shaken, more so from my knowledge of his secrets than from fear or anger.

"I don't know who you are, but you need to leave," he tells me, making it very clear—in his mind anyway—just who exactly is in charge of the situation.

Curious. I sense power and control as prevalent themes with this man.

"I will leave," I reply coyly, "just as soon as I—"

There is no time to finish because in a single fluid motion he takes the revolver out and aims it at me.

"NOW," he says.

I sigh deeply and smile the way one smiles politely at a stale joke.

"Must we really do things this way?" I ask tiredly.

He is obviously unamused and I hear a loud cracking noise and the echoing ricochet of a bullet against the floor. "I won't miss next time," his wide eyes tell me.

It really takes no effort at all because I only need a few moments of concentration. The Pedophile has made up his mind to kill me, already fabricating the story he will tell the police. He is ready to pull the trigger, when he shrieks in pain. In the sudden shock he grips the pistol's hilt. This is a mistake, as it is now glowing red with heat.

He drops it and it clatters to the floor, misfiring. He has ducked behind the counter and it sounds as if he is swearing in low tones. I begin to approach the counter when I feel a cool draft…a curious thing, as the door is still shut.

An instant later I am slammed backwards by an invisible force. When I stand, my head is singing, and I feel something warm trickle from my nose…blood. The old man peeks from behind the counter to see if all is well before he stands to leer at me. It seems I've underestimated this man.

"You idiot!" he shouts at me as if he's scolding a wayward teenager. "Did you think I'd run this shop for fifty years without learning a thing?!"

He doesn't wait for me to answer.

"You'll live a long time regretting this day you monster!" he snarls at me.

I snicker as I wipe at my nose with the back of my hand. He doesn't know it yet, but he's raised the fight in me. I begin to gather energies around me, but as I do, a bright ring appears encircling me, growing brighter by the minute. I notice the man is laughing, but he shouldn't, for I know the workings of this particular spell.

"Anything you try to use will only strengthen your prison you demon!" he spits at me.

I abandon the attempt and the ring fades, yet it does not disappear. We glare at each other in silence a long time before he begins to speak.

"Now," he says—a bit shakily from the excitement, but trying to regain his composure, trying to establish the fact that he is the superior one in this situation. "The question is," he continues, trying it seems to sound very educated, "what shall we do with you my dear." As he finishes, he nods his head towards me in a mocking way. "Perhaps," he says licking his lips, enjoying each moment of delusory power over me, "I should send you back where you came from." He pauses, owl eyes calculating. "Or," he begins again, "perhaps I can coax you to show me your true form."

He suddenly chuckles, but it has the giddy edge of one intoxicated…overstimulated with the notion that he can do anything his heart desires, and I can do nothing to stop him. His expression changes, and he smiles the smile of someone who has come to a difficult, but pleasing decision. He hobbles away from the counter, and I hear the sound of jingling keys and then the click of what I can only assume to be an ancient lock. Then comes the creak of what must be an equally ancient cabinet. He seems to be grunting, and hefting something heavy. Momentarily he comes back into the front room and lays a thick, large-sized book on the counter. It has the appearance of many other books of his—old and insignificantly uninteresting—yet this one is perhaps the most dangerous in his collection for it specializes in the raising, binding, creation, and control of demons…among other things. I roll my eyes at my own foolishness.

Looking slightly deeper into this being, I detect hints of the sick and perverted things which bring him pleasure and it is enough to make me shudder. It appears he is perhaps a borderline necrophiliac as well. At the counter, he is nonchalantly flipping pages, in no particular hurry, and indeed acting as if he's forgotten me.

"Aha!" he cries triumphantly, raising his head to peer at me through slitted eyes. "Just what I was looking for," he says in a tone reeking of mock sweetness.

"Oh really," I reply sarcastically.

He pauses and frowns at this, unamused by my lack of concern...my audacity to belittle him.

"That's right my dear, enjoy it while you can, for soon you will be mine!"

I don't like the way he finishes.

"You don't know how long I've waited for this," he says, almost hastily, "to have my very own demon...to use as I please! You'll regret the day you ever set foot in here my dear, yes...I'll make sure of that."

This has gone far enough. Perhaps I've already wasted too much time.

"I'm sorry to disappoint you," I say, focusing intently on his eyes, "but I am not a demon."

These last words he hears as if they are spoken right into his ear, as they should, for I am behind him. He jumps, and in his confusion loses his balance and stumbles to the floor. He looks at me in disbelief, the memory of his triumph—the still glowing ring where I stood just a moment before—shattering like the frail and dusty tomes left to rot and waste away on his dark shelves.

"What—what are you?!" he nearly shrieks, trying to scoot away from me before I hurt him even more.

I consider his question briefly, and in answer I sweep the demonology book into my left arm.

"I am someone who cares for you," I say placing

my right palm upon it. It immediately leaps into flames, "someone who cares more than you will ever know," I finish, meeting his eyes once again.

The tears I see coming from them now are a mixture of fear and awe and anger at his own humiliation, and it seems he's realized for the first time just how insignificant a creature he really is. The flames in my arms die down and I brush away the ashes, scattering them upon the ground between us. He is trembling, unable to take his eyes from me...afraid to honestly, for he feels that in doing so he will lose his life. I smile at such simple mindedness, for I am not here to kill him.

"Please give me the book," I intone to him gently, lovingly, like the first woman who ever showed him kindness...before he moved to this city, before he knew the intoxication of the ways of the Dark.

"It is in my bedroom," he tells me meekly.

I smile...truly smile, and move closer to him. I smell so sweet to him now and seem so beautiful, for he is locked within my eyes. I kneel beside him, delicately shifting the folds of my skirt as not to dirty it.

"Thank you," I tell him, and then I kiss him—once—upon his forehead.

His eyes slide shut and the air rushes out of his lungs in a haphazard sigh. All sense of balance vacates his body and his head thuds heavily on the floor behind him as he falls. I regard him. Perhaps in a different life, I would pity him. I angle my body to peer closer, but my senses scream. My eyes dart upwards, and I stand to my feet quickly. Something is wrong.

****

3

I don't know how long I sat there staring into nothing after she left. My tears for him were wasted. I had wept so much already...too much. This much was apparent even to me, but the problem was, I still loved him.

"Oh Eath. Eath, Eath, Eath," I sighed bending over; shaking my head in cupped hands.

Why can't he...how can he not understand? Why does he continue to do these things that only end up hurting people...people who don't deserve to be hurt? And an even better question is: why do I do nothing to stop him?

Even as I ask myself such a thing, the answer comes—unbidden and automatic. It stares me in the face. Indeed, I've already named it. But love? Love does not give license for these deeds...no.

Though my tears have ebbed, I feel as if they'll begin anew, and I remind myself once again that I've wept far too much for him and the things he's done. Suddenly, I begin to feel very angry. I wish I'd never met him, and that none of this had happened. But even as I think it, I know it is a lie...and this makes me even angrier at myself.

I sniffle and sigh and stretch and stand. How long will I chase after him...allow him to pull me along behind him like a dog?

I hear the kettle, still shrieking...echoing the sentiment in my heart almost perfectly. I have to be strong. I make my way to the kitchen and to the stove. I turn the knob quickly and the flame goes out. The kettle's song softens before fading away to nothing but tempered hisses and gurgling.

I reach for the cup, by the window sill as always, to find that it is not there. I pause, frowning. The breeze rests against my hand in reply. I wonder has she caught up with him yet. As I think about this, a surge of emotion begins to well up, and I am angry again. How can I still love the man who left me blinded! Though again, as the thought arises, I know that it is not completely accurate, for I am still able to see...after a fashion.

I concentrate for a moment, and then see my cup resting behind me on the opposite counter, each immaculate detail laid out before me in what I would like to call my mind's eye...but I know somehow that my new sense of sight is not the same as the images I see when I use my mind.

I sigh and close the window. Then I lock it. Perhaps he moved it to prevent himself from breaking it as he fled? It's strange to imagine he would offer me this simple courtesy, but the fact remains that the cup is not broken. Perhaps he only moved it to decrease the likelihood of detection. I nod involuntarily, making a noise. This is far more likely. Had it fallen and broken, it would have caught her attention.

I am unsettled. Why do I care? I know exactly why I care. I don't want her to hurt him...even after what he's done. But at the same time, I don't feel as if it's him that she's truly after. Maybe I should be alarmed. Eathan was obviously far beyond that point for him to actually use that old escape plan. I catch myself smirking in spite of myself at the memory of the day he brought it up. I would distract whoever it was, and he would use the fire escape. I'd openly laughed.

"Who you be runnin' with to gotta have an escape plan?" I'd quipped.

He failed to understand what I found so amusing, and launched into an explanation about how beavers always made sure to create several doors to their dens, and so why not emulate the best planners in nature.

But the thing is, somehow I know...just like I knew that she came here about the mandala. I frown again, an idea suddenly occurring to me. Whatever it is that she is here to do will most likely mean that his mandala will be removed. This in and of itself is probably a good thing. But the books in his place...I have to make sure that they are kept safe.

As I feel the cool air caress my face, I begin to feel better. Who would have known that a brisk walk would do me this much good? The feeling, however, diminishes as I grow nearer to my destination. I climb the stairs towards Eathan's apartment and reach the landing. I've walked this route so many times I see it in my dreams. I don't even need my stick to come here... though I brought it along anyway. In a strange sort of way, it provides me comfort. It reminds me of what it means to have someone there watching out for you, and helping you to remain on the path you've intended to take.

This time, as I enter the landing, something seems different. I'm not exactly sure if it's the strange and empty smell that's hanging in the air or the feeling of hopelessness that pervades my midsection as I face his door. I take my key from my pocket and slide it into the lock; turning it. I open the door; standing awkwardly just before the threshold. It is very silent here, and I'm sure I'm alone...yet.... I half laugh from my nose. Was I expecting he'd be here, that I could tell him I loved him and he'd better well love me in return or stay the hell away? Did I really have the gall to end things with him here of all places, where this whole thing began? And now, of all times? Now...when something has come through into our world and he's in trouble? He's in over his head. He has to be...though, he's never said so. After all, this is the reason *she* came. Of that, I am certain.

I step in and close the door behind me without bothering to lock it. I won't be here that long. Even as I make my way towards the living room, I detect muted hues of indigo and violet. Their source is the places on the floor where his mandala is still intact. Part of me is still in awe at the novelty of this way of perceiving things. Though I can't "see" it per se, I can sense it. I know it is there. And somehow since I can sense it, I know exactly where it is located and what it looks like...even its colors.

The colors are strange in that they seem darker today. I wonder does that mean their strength is fading. I pause and kneel to trace the space above one of the mandala's words, and the word becomes brighter. Already, I feel its energy rushing up around me and through me. This one is for strength.

I turn my attention towards Eathan's mounds upon mounds of books, and already the lines leap and dance towards me beckoning. I navigate easily though the mist of words, choosing promising specimens here and there. I slip my backpack on so that it is hanging from my chest, and slip the books I've chosen inside. I work quickly and efficiently. I can't lose these.

When he first came to me, when he asked for my help, I thought it would be a simple matter of translation. I thought perhaps he would need some help decoding. I had no idea that he would bring so much knowledge with him. I don't even know where he got these books. Though I can only begin to imagine the depths of what Eathan's done, I know that she—whoever, or whatever it is that she is—will end it. He is many things, but there are too many good books here to lose...some in languages the world has long forgotten...or never seen. There were many I certainly hadn't. Not even with all those hours of university linguistics research. I shift the contents of the backpack to make more room when I notice the change in temperature. Eathan's apartment was never very well insulated, but now it is cold. Had I been smarter, or more experienced rather, I would have left that instant. Instead, I turn my head from side to side, listening for the tell-tale signs of entry into the apartment.

My heart flutters. Eathan? In the next instant, my eyes narrow. Surely he wouldn't be stupid enough to come back here. Wouldn't this be the first place she would come searching for him? Something is definitely off, but before I can ponder this fact any further, my attention is drawn towards the floor again. The mandala's colors are no longer mere wisps of shimmering lights, but are now a strong and solid glow. In fact, to my eye which is not an eye, many of the letters appear to be dancing.

I draw closer. Is it just my imagination, or are the colors getting brighter as well? I squat. It is beautiful—as I have never seen it before—but also, something tells me it is the sign of nothing good. I shake my head and frown. Something about this seems familiar. Memories of that awful night come rushing back to me now. I don't like this at all.

It is after I stand that I hear her voice.

"We have to leave," she says urgently.

The sudden exchange startles me, and I jump; arms wrapping tightly around the bookbag so that none its contents fall out. I open my mouth to answer, but begin to hear something akin to a high-pitched whine. She swears and then growls at me.

"Get away from the mandala, now! Don't touch it!"

I retreat to the nearest enclave behind one of the stacks of papers and books. Though my hands are shaking, I still absentmindedly grab at whatever is around me: loose papers, notebooks, pamphlets, books, anything.

"Stop moving!" she snaps authoritatively.

The whining grows louder until it seems that the room itself is its source. The mandala is blazing. Though I know the markings are still on the floor, its aura has risen higher, and seems to be both expanding and solidifying. It is also generating heat. It has to be, for I can feel it reaching out into the room and reacting against the cold.

Its letters continue dancing and spinning. The colors grow more vivid, and seem so much brighter now. I know I should be alarmed, but this is amazing, and I begin to weep. This is nothing like that awful night. I wish I could touch it. I wish I could hold just one small part of it. I wish I could let something so incredibly beautiful be part of me. Then maybe I could be beautiful too.

The walls begin to vibrate as if someone is pounding on them, and I hear something unlike anything I've ever heard before. There is a rip. That's the only way to describe it. The mandala expands once more, and it is as if everything within and around it is jostled with a violent whipping.

She is muttering...speaking...chanting? I hear her voice transform and it sounds as if there are many voices. Their tones and intonations grate upon my eardrums. Then I hear something that I can only describe as otherworldly. It is a scream. But it is far more than any Earthly scream, for it draws terror to it like the moon draws the tides.

<*Shut up*> I hear her voice directly in my mind, commanding and firm, <*or It will find you and consume you*>.

I close my mouth. I hadn't realized I was screaming too. There is light brighter than any sun I've ever seen... and juxtaposed against it is darkness...a living darkness so black and full of malice that my body immediately spasms to spur me into flight.

<*Be still!*>, she commands, <*Are you trying to die?*>

The living darkness has gone quiet. I don't know

how, but I know that It knows It is not alone. It will find me. It will find me! It will find me, good God almighty It will find me! I have to get out. I have to get out!

It releases another otherworldly scream, yet this one is different. Now more than ever, I wish I had the ability to see through my eyes like a normal person; like I could before that awful night, because I can see this living darkness's scream. There are tendrils of darkness that are not quite darkness that wriggle and writhe within and upon sound. It is revolting, but at the same time I can sense a very precise and organized intelligence. Perhaps it is this quality which is most disturbing. It's searching for something. How do I shut my new eyes... my eyes that are no eyes?

I sense a shift in movement, and there is a sound like thunder. There is a bright flash, and then the room quakes as if struck with powerful force. I hear a series of pops, straining cracking noises, and loud wooden creaks of protest. The walls and the floor, as well as the ceiling have begun to collapse. Books tumble over onto me and I feel myself begin to slide forward towards the mandala. I try to scoot away, but cannot. Suddenly, she is beside me again.

"It's too late now," she says.

I open my mouth to speak, yet I feel the wind knocked out of me.

There is silence. Indeed, I am not certain the term is adequate, for what I experience is not the cessation of noise, or its absence. It is as if in this place, sound has never existed. I feel alone, and slightly cold, and though I know it seems silly, I can no longer tell which way is up. I know I am no longer falling. I am not sliding towards the mandala. I can no longer see it. I can no longer see anything. Perhaps this is what it is like to be truly blind? I exist in this state for some time it seems—though to be honest I have no idea how long—and then suddenly feel a hard, wooden floor rushing up to meet my knees. The bookbag's straps slide from around my shoulders and it falls from my chest onto the floor. I push it aside, take a breath—air ripping into my lungs like a starving animal—and then gag. As I lurch and struggle to breathe, I feel her beside me.

"Are you injured?" she asks, almost accusatory in her tone.

It takes a moment before I can manage to register that she's asked me a question, let alone a sputter of a reply.

"What just happened?" I cough out, "Where are we? What was that?"

I gag again, this time very near to emptying the contents of my stomach.

"Breathe deeply and slowly," she commands.

I try to do as she says, but my body wracks with a fit of coughing, and I lower myself so that my elbows are also touching the ground along with my knees. Then I lower my head into my hands. This helps to soothe me, and presently, my breathing returns to normal. I still feel shaky, and my eyes are squeezed closed. But this time, my voice is more stable as I ask her again.

"What was that?"

I hear her step closer, and then squat next to me. Part of me already knows the answer. But I have to hear her say it before I am willing to recognize it as the truth.

"That was the Beast that Idiot has brought into your world," she replies, coldly, "with the aid of the mandala," her tone changes to one of rebuke now, "that you helped him create."

I take a deep breath and shake my head. "I didn't help him create the mandala. I only rendered rough translations for his mantras."

"It is the same thing!" she roars out at me.

"That thing...that Beast...It was searching for something," I say, ignoring her. "Tell me that It wasn't looking for Eathan," I utter, voice suddenly warbling and threatening to break.

She makes no reply.

"You have to help him!" I hear my voice cry out, ashamed of its inflections and the modulations of its accompanying tears.

Still, she makes no reply. I open my eyes, sit up and seize her hands so quickly, so tightly, that I can feel her jump in surprise. But it is I who am surprised, for in that moment I can see her true form. I see her many faces. I see her many arms, and the implements she wields in each of her many hands. Her aura's light equals that which shone from the mandala, but unlike the form she wears on this plane and the personality she dons to accompany it, it emanates a profoundly deep and boundless compassion. I gasp and hear another cry escape my throat before releasing her hands just as quickly as I'd grabbed them.

"I—I'm sorry," I utter, sitting back, wide-eyed in spite of myself.

"Don't be," she replies darkly.

And then, she is gone.

****

4

In the time it takes to breathe, I return to the clearing. The Coward...is gone. I growl, gritting my teeth, stamping my foot, and clenching my fist in irritation. How is it that this simpleton can be so incredibly skilled at fleeing? And how is it that I continue to underestimate him?

I move closer to the protective ward—which is still intact—and see an inert body where The Coward should be. Curious. It is obvious by the state of decay, that the being who once wore this form has departed it many months prior. I look closer, and I see what appears to be a hole in the earth. If it were smaller, and if circumstances were different, it might be mistaken for a rabbit's burrowing hole.

I focus my inner eye upon our surroundings, and am presently rewarded with enlightening information. Not far from here is a cemetery. This would explain the body. It is obvious that The Coward still has a few tricks up his sleeve—including the ability to raise the dead. How much did The Pedophile teach him? Or— and I frown as I consider the notion—did he undertake the effort to learn such a thing on his own?

I step closer, and kneel. I should perhaps be more concerned, and I will definitely be more careful with him from now on.

I raise my hand, just about to dissolve the ward, when something catches my eye. A faint glimmering of light has attached itself to the body. I use my inner sight to look closer, and see that the body is indeed still animated…partially at least. The energy signature surrounding it mimics that of The Coward nearly perfectly. Where he learned such things, I do not know. I shake my head. There is another tendril of light which goes from the body, and connects itself to the boundaries of the ward. I see. He has connected the ward to this body. Very clever indeed. He does not realize it, but he has actually done something useful. He has very crudely masked his energy signature.

With the ward in place, the Beast shall remain confused and unable to find him. And the new ward should remain intact as long as the body to which it is attached—false energy signature and all—remains as it is. It is just as well. Let him think he has outsmarted me and that he has a head start. It will give me the time I need to return and retrieve The Pedophile's book before it can fall into the hands of those whose ignorance leads them into danger. I smirk, and rise to my feet. Perhaps subduing this Eathan will be more enjoyable than I imagined.

Offering

Offering

It wasn't his Sacred Wand Of Light...that most sacred pathway between this world and his. Of course I could see it...sense it...feel the way it strained against the taut purple fabric of innermost garments...taste the heady aroma wafting from the fine hairs which billowed and blossomed like the roots of a plant which dared to burst through the concrete, and feel the budding dampness of those dangling, pendulous fruits like smooth and sensuously glistening avocado seeds. No, that wasn't what drew me to him. He called my **name**.

That deep, browned skin...those sharp, green eyes...and that tuft of chest hair that billowed from the front of his shirt...he was a beautiful man, that much was apparent. His hair was long, and black, and thick and somehow powerfully strong. He was dressed simply enough—a slightly wrinkled dress shirt and trousers that appeared to be a touch more elegant than blue jeans. He wore riding boots...dusty, and worn, and somehow seeming ancient. Though it was also clear he cherished them dearly.

When I first heard him, it gave me pause. Not the fact that he called, for many do. It was the *way* he called out to me...*sought* me, stretched his awareness through the cosmos to *find* me. It was an ancient name...not the common titles and honourifics pilfered from lust dulled tongues in search of simple favours. And at this hour... that was unusual indeed. Had it been dusk, had it been the depths of the night, I would have paid little notice.

But *now*? Now with the sun risen an hour prior, now with the creatures of the day up and tending to their tasks, now in the brazen, illuminating light of morning…to call my name *now*? What was *this*?

When he spoke, I felt the depths of desire from deep within his heart. I felt the promise of life surging and coursing through his veins and out into the world like the rapids of a raging torrented river…a flower unfurling its blossoms.

He was on one knee, and had lit the candle. He had the apricots, the plum wine, the fruitcake, the pomegranate and the marigolds. I could have left then. I could have left then and decided what to do about it later. I could have refused, or denied him. I could have ignored him altogether. But he had the offerings…**all** of them. When was the last time anyone left me my complete offerings? How long had it been since any took the time, the care, and the consideration to understand what brought *me* pleasure? I stayed and drew closer. Of course he never knew—he couldn't feel me. He was praying out loud.

"Thank you," he whispered, "thank you for this day, and the joy you bring to my life. Thank you for imbuing me with the perception to understand your love."

He slowly unbuttoned and removed his shirt.

"Thank you for ever reaching your hands through the darkness of our hearts to find us."

His hands brushed along his breast and down his torso, teasing all his thick, dark, wiry and fragrant tuft of mossy-soft hair along his sternum.

"Thank you for remembering us, though so many neglect you."

He removed his boots, then unbuttoned and removed his trousers.

"Thank you for holding us, and endeavouring to show us who we truly are."

I blessed him. He felt me then, for the first time, registering my presence with a shudder.

I began inside the deepest part of his beautifully blossomed fertile fruit, and expanded outwards. He felt the energy of Life welling throughout and beneath him, before it rose to envelop his abdomen, chest, head, and wash over his entire body with its Light. The erection surprised him. Later, the tell-tale stain of seminal fluid on his underwear would fascinate and amaze him, and he would continue to pray to me. Each morning he would rise, stretch and sing my ancient name to the clouds, trace my sacred syllables across his supple skin, see the world through his single eye as it showered his seed in offering...all in my name. **My** name. Not my *true* name—no—but a name so ancient it was all but forgotten as the first of mankind forged its way towards darker futures with the gift of flame.

For the next three weeks I hear him daily. I smile. I send pleasure, warmth, and Love. He feels them, and is satisfied. This, I know. He offers thanks. Then, it is silent. I think nothing of it, it happens often enough. Human beings are so busy these days. It's not like I don't understand what it means to be human...I was one myself not all that long ago. Besides, I had countless others to tend to. What was one less voice among millions?

But then, five months later, I hear him…or more accurately, I sense him. I feel something akin to jagged glass ripping through skin, and feel a painful wail shaped in the words that form my name. This is bad. I know it is him. His special scent comes to my awareness the second after I feel him call out to me, and I go to him.

It is unusual for me. I like to remain unseen. I do my duties silently, and in ways that most will remain unaware of. But something about this night is different, and I appear to him in physical form. He is startled at first…but only for a few moments. He falls at my feet weeping, pleading for me to interfere. He falls to my feet pleading for my mercy. He falls to my feet pleading for me to do something to undo what has happened. And though something tells me I will not like what I see when I do so, I look into the cause of his sorrow.

Blood.

The first image that assails my awareness is blood… bright, and vivid…fecund and humid smelling…dripping into the water the way tears do…unapologetically, and unashamed. I do not need to look further to guess what I will find next, but I continue to watch in time with his sobs. He rushes his wife to the hospital, but they are too late. Though it would provide them no comfort to be sure, this was the Being which was to be their child's choice. The doctors, and the nurses all fall back on their training, and do the best they can to provide explanations, and offer care. To their credit— though many of them are thinking it—they do not utter trite and well-intentioned insults such as: "But you are still young, you'll have many chances more" or "you can try again."

They are devastated.

"Please," he begs me, "please", he sobs.

His words are incomprehensible but I understand him perfectly; for I know his very thoughts and emotions. How do I tell him that this is beyond my power? How do I tell him that in this matter, even I have no sway? How could he possibly begin to understand that though I act as conduit for Life, I do not command it? And now, how can I ever justify answering another prayer like his again?

"I am not The Giver Of Life," I say to him, and he sniffles, looking at me as if he doesn't understand.

I wish I weren't who I am. I wish these talents…these responsibilities were not mine. I wish that I could return to that day that I thought as a foolish boy that I could seduce a God, and be loved eternal. You may bestow your titles, you may praise and flatter me with accolades and attention, but how can I pretend to be enlightened when—for all my power—I can do nothing to help those in the midst of true suffering? Why must the pleasure I seek to give be balanced by death and pain?

It is then once again that I bless him. He feels me then, like the first time, registering my presence with a shudder. I began inside the deepest part of his beautiful heart, and expanded outwards. He feels the energy of LOVE welling throughout and beneath him, before it rises to envelop his abdomen, chest, head, and wash over his entire body with its Light. The joy surprises him. Later, this memory will bring him tears, but he will continue to pray. Each morning he will rise, stretch and sing the song of his love to the clouds, trace its sacred syllables across his supple skin, see the world through his single eye and hold his seed in offering within...all in his name. **His** name. Not his *true* name—no—but a name so powerful he would scarcely remember as he forged his way from grief towards brighter futures with a gift...the gift of love that knows no time...the knowledge of Life that knows no end...and the awareness of his love...rippling and radiating throughout the world; coming back to bless him in return.

www.ingramcontent.com/pod-product-compliance
Lightning Source LLC
Chambersburg PA
CBHW051144020726
47501CB00005B/1666